LORENZ TRAVELING DIARIES

by DRAEGON GREY

CONTRIBUTORS:

Angela Thang
Editor

Diego Moreno
Illustrator

LOLORIC

Black
Sea

BEXO

PARSI
OCEAN

Stone Sea

BABEL
OCEAN

CALEB

Caleb Gulf

Gulf

FST PULP

Published by Failed Saving Throw

Forbidden Sea

— Second Edition —

Copyright © 2012 by DRAEGON GREY

9 78-1935582700

TIVER

FST PULP

Red Sea

Der
Bay

A very big Thanks to all of those that have helped in the development of this Novella.

Without this help, this would have taken much longer and been much more difYcult.

Additionally, this is also in Memorandum of

Keith B. Vines

Who contributed to the Yrst version of this book.

He will be missed.

BOOKS by Draegon Grey

Lorenz Traveling Diaries

E.O.T.W.

Spectrum

Check out the new Lorenz adventure "Rise of Davian"

DRAEGON GREY

CONTENTS

FROM THE DIARY OF ADVENTURING LORENZ

This is the incredible tale of Lorenz, a lonely young boy living in the inner city. Lorenz's life would never be the same because of a strange and magical gem that he stumbles in across one summer's day.

This is his story—the story of how an unusual world filled with intrigue, excitement, and unpredictable thrills wound up changing his life. In this new world, he would learn, excel and grow from an inexperienced boy into a young man.

Sit back, dig in and enjoy the ride. You never know what might be coming around the corner.

CHAPTER ONE

My name is Lorenzo. I'm a twelve year old African American boy living in a large city in the East Coast. Distant grey skyscrapers lined the hazy horizon where my brother Darius and I lived with relatives in their home in the suburbs. I was currently staying with my mom's older sister Georgia and her boyfriend Wes.

My mother worked and lived in a different city, working long hours in odd shifts at various part-time jobs, trying to save up to make a better living for my brother and me—a home to call our own, a nice school, books, college fund, all that stuff.

She was able to visit us frequently, driving over as often as she could to spend time with us on the weekends. If she didn't have the time to see us in person, she made sure to call on a regular basis. My little brother seemed more or less indifferent about it. He was happy enough staying with Aunt Georgia and I could see him growing distant from Mom over time. Maybe he thought that since we didn't live with her, that she didn't love us, but it was clear to me that our welfare was very important to her, even if she wasn't able to take care of us.

My mom was all I had after my father had left when I was very young— young enough that I couldn't even remember what he looked like. Sometimes I thought I'd remembered a faint flicker of his face, but they might have been just false memories from all the times I'd stared longingly at photos of him and Mom, as if all my longing and hoping would bring them back together somehow. I missed Mom terribly and her love for me was as comforting and warm as the sun, compared to the grudging care I received from my loathing aunt, who seemed to hate my mother and me.

The house we lived in was a big two story home with four bedrooms. Along with a front and back porch, there was a basement and an unkempt backyard full of weeds. Georgia and Wes also kept several cats, which I had to help them with on many occasions. To no surprise, they always saved the dirty jobs for me.

Even though my brother and I lived together, we weren't very close. As we got older, we rarely hung out or played with each other, especially after we moved in with our aunt. Since Darius got along better with our relatives, he was always able to get away with breaking the rules. He'd break curfew, skip dinner, leave the lights on or water running, and he'd never get a word about it. Plus, he'd never invite me to hang out with his friends. I resented Aunt Georgia's deliberate favoritism and my brother's stuck-up companions, which left me not wanting to spend much time with any of them.

Those days, I had many problems with the way other people would treat me, and it wasn't just at home. I liked to be left alone most times since, usually, interaction with another person involved either me being bullied or otherwise being actively disliked or excluded. Like most other children too timid to stand up for themselves, I had an assortment of bullies that I had to contend with. They seemed to have nothing better to do than to try their hardest to make my life miserable, and sometimes it was even unbearable.

Many days, I saw varying degrees of violence at school. Bloody fistfights between students were common, egged on by the hooting and hollering of the rabid little on-lookers. The adults weren't much better; a lot of parents yelled and cursed at their kids, right in public, about some issue or other from home. I tried to comfort myself in thinking that I only had to endure this scene for one more year before moving onto middle school. Needless to say, the elementary school wasn't any more warm or welcoming than my Aunt Georgia's house.

To clear my head of all the awful feelings from the hate and anger constantly around me, I enjoyed playing games outside. They were just mindless "little kid" games, but I liked it that way. It was fun and kept my mind off things. Since Georgia didn't let me roam around, I would usually play on the sidewalk directly in front of my house, with various other neighborhood friends around my age.

Hide-and-seek, tag, and one-two-three red light were some of the simple games we played together to pass the time. I would've liked to walk to a friend's house now and then to play video games or watch TV with the others, but Georgia didn't allow me to visit anyone. Unlike Darius, I was tethered to the house and its immediate proximity.

Not to say that I never got to roam around myself. There were days, especially if none of my friends were outside and Aunt Georgia wasn't at home, that I could go out alone, exploring the immediate neighborhood to distract myself and get away from everything—my spiteful household, the puerile bullies, or having to be constantly grounded for stupid things.

One warm Sunday afternoon, I decided to explore a nearby alley, behind a neighbor's house, which exited out onto the main street. This bright, sunny, summer day, the sun was shining strong in the sky. The temperature was about only 88 degrees, but it was very humid, so it felt much more intense and sweat coated my skin. I was dressed in a blue and white striped polo shirt and blue jeans, with the new white and black tennis shoes that my mother had bought me.

The narrow alley was lined with old, dark red, rectangular bricks. It continued west into the next block, extending from one street to another. In the middle of the alley was an intersection going north, which went past my aunt's backyard. On each side were the garages or backyards of the various homes in the neighborhood.

Most of the backyards had old wooden porches with stairs leading down to ground level, protected by chain-link fences or gates with padlocks. Some of the chain-link fences that separated the properties of each house were lined with razor wire on top, to deter would-be thieves. Other homes had busted up jalopies rusted in place in their driveways and most homes had vicious guard dogs that would bark fiercely whenever someone walked anywhere nearby.

While walking north, past some of these noisy dogs, looking down idly at the cracked red bricks and kicking stray pebbles, I came upon something small that seemed to glow oddly in the dim alleyway. Whatever it was, it was partially buried under some dirt and debris and it emitted a sharp, bright, purple light.

"What's that?" I wondered aloud.

Thinking it might be a lost cell phone or portable game console, I stopped and knelt down to get a closer look. I pushed aside the grody old candy wrappers and empty cans and dug it out from under the grass growing on the clumps of dirt stuck to it. Lo and behold, lying amongst the weeds growing in the cracks was this beautiful, sparkling gem, shining brightly on the ground. It was lying hidden against a five foot fence, flanked by patches of crabgrass and dandelion. I looked to see if anyone was around before reaching for it. To my delight, I was all alone. Eagerly, I reached down and carefully picked up the object.

"Gem" wasn't the right word exactly, but it was the best word I could think of to describe it. It had a distinct royal purple color with solid gold trimming and was shaped like a small pyramid. The surface was glossy and smooth to the touch, with strange engravings etched into it. There was a noticeable narrow gap between the top of the pyramid and the rest of the gem, which appeared to be movable joint. I examined every inch of this treasure in amazement, as I had never seen anything like it.

I said breathily to myself, "Wow..."

I knew that this was special. The way it shone and glowed—it wasn't just some toy you'd buy at Wal-Mart. It was otherworldly. I wished that there was someone I that trusted who I could show it to or ask about it, but I knew that if I took this to my relatives, they would just take it from me. If I asked my friends, they might want to take it as well. Giving it more thought, I decided that I needed to keep this mysterious artifact a secret.

I decided to go and find someplace safe, where no one would find me or bother me. I figured that Aunt Georgia's basement was as good a place as any. Since it was dusty, and chock full of junk and mildew, no one ever came down here. I snuck into my aunt's basement through the backyard as furtively as possible. I was all alone except for the piles of stained cardboard boxes, broken bicycles, and splintered crates. The old boxes and crates were filled to the brim with useless or forgotten odds and ends. There, in this dim room, I felt safe. No one would try to take the gem while I sat on the dusty cement stairs in the dark.

It was still and quiet down in the basement… besides the fact that I could hear my aunt and her boyfriend upstairs moving around. They were oblivious to the fact that I was so close by, leaning against the basement door. While sitting there, hearing the muffled voices and footsteps, I forgot about the gem for a moment while I listened to what they were saying. Their obnoxiously loud voices carried easily through the thin walls.

"Where's that boy, Lorenzo?" Georgia's voice rang out. "He run off, up to no good again, I'll bet! He ain't even cleaned out the litter box, like I told him to, the lazy brat! If he's gonna be so useless around here, his ma oughta just take him back, if she weren't such a deadweight herself-"

I stopped listening, squeezing my eyes shut and covering my ears. Still, I heard my aunt and Wes agree about how I shouldn't be around, all the "trouble" I caused, and how much "work" it was for them to care for me. They complained about how my mother should get a real job and take care of me herself. They called her irresponsible and grumbled about all the toil they had to endure with no extra pay to compensate.

In reality, my mother was a considerate woman and sent them money frequently to help pay for our living expenses. Whatever money they received from my mom, however, the amount they received was never enough to please them and they always dismissed it.

After hearing the two of them toss around insults for many minutes, I couldn't stand it anymore. Feeling thoroughly miserable, I buried my face in my hands, close to tears as my stomach wrenched. I tried to refocus my attention on the gem I had found earlier. Hearing their loathsome words reminded me of how much I hated it here. How I wished I could live with my mother again, or at least live with someone who really cared about me!

I went back to examining the gem, focusing particularly on the articulation on the top. It looked like it could twist. While closely eyeing it, I placed my right index finger and thumb around the tip, turning it slightly until I felt it click and move.

Something inside me must have been changing because I began to feel different. Unable to understand or describe what was going on, I just knew something strange was happening. It started with the pit of my stomach tingling intensely.

I didn't know what to do or what was occurring. It was dim in the basement, but suddenly it seemed like I was falling into absolute darkness. I couldn't see anything! I started yelling at the top of my lungs, panicked, hoping for someone, anyone, to help me. While plummeting, I squeezed my eyes shut, terrified. I had no idea where I was going.

It must have only been seconds, but with my heart pounding in my throat, it felt like ages. Before I realized it, I had landed on what felt like solid ground. I hit the ground feet first, but promptly dropped onto my butt from the rough momentum of the fall. I was stunned, but glad I wasn't hurt. When I initially opened my eyes, they weren't yet clearly focused and it was too bright to see much of anything.

When my vision adjusted, I found that I was surrounded by tall brown grass and the ground I was now sitting on was covered with dried fallen leaves. The gloomy basement I was in just a moment ago was gone.

Shading my eyes with my hand, I could see what looked like a forest, but the trees weren't anything at all familiar like oak, maple or beech. Instead, the forest was filled with enormous trees with lobed broad green leaves, the likes of which I had never seen before. These trees had to be at least 400 feet tall! They were so high that they seemed to reach the sky. The branches were amazingly wide and thick and hung down low. I had never been this close to a real forest before, but I had doubts that any normal forest looked like this.

After staring in bewilderment at the trees, I looked around to see if there were any people or animals. I didn't see anything. It seemed that I was all alone in the middle of this giant forest, so I began to stand myself up from the grass where I was sitting. When I looked at my hands pressing on the ground in the effort to stand, I realized that my hands were different. They seemed much bigger than usual, but not as if they were hurt or swollen from the fall.

I brought my hands to my face in surprise, to feel if everything there was all right. I took my right hand and rubbed it across my cheek, nose and lips, feeling the slight prickle of mysterious stubble. Concerned, I felt the rest of my upper body, all of which felt normal, just larger. Relieved, I looked down at my feet and realized that I was wearing completely different clothing. My feet were also bigger and I was wearing new shoes. Bigger hands and bigger feet and I seemed taller too!

"What happened?" I said to myself in shock. It was like I had suddenly grown up into an adult man.

The clothing I was wearing seemed to be made of a fabric that I was not familiar with. I was wearing pants made of a thick, heavy cloth, yet it was soft enough to be maneuverable and felt very durable. The shirt and jacket on my body had the same texture. The color scheme of my new garb seemed to be a stylish combination of copper and jet black.

Laying my hands on the mysterious clothing, I wondered where they could have come from. The shoes were warm and comfortable, not like regular sneakers, but more like tough leather boots for hiking—like the expensive boots you'd find at a sporting goods store, except more rustic.

I checked my pockets and found nothing but the gem, which I was relieved to find resting safely inside. It that thing brought me here, it could probably get me back, from... wherever I was. I then looked up at the rest of my surroundings.

The sky was amazingly clear with patches of variously shaped, fluffy, white clouds. There were large orange circles, which looked like hazy setting suns, shining brightly in the sky, except that there were two of them. The air was crisp and refreshing and felt warm on my skin. The scents of pine and wood drifted on a gentle breeze. The sounds around me were that of leaves rustling, and birds and insects chirping in every direction, even though I couldn't see them. As I continued to soak in the surroundings, I turned in a full circle, looking in the directions that I imagined were north, east, south and west.

I saw countless trees, but in the northwest direction, I noticed one huge tree with reddish-brown bark that had a large hole in it. This hole was big enough for an adult to easily fit through. It was almost like a cave, except that it had a light coming from inside. The opening stretched from the foot of the tree to about seven feet high and about several feet wide, forming a doorway.

The light coming from the tree was bright, even in the sunlight. It felt as bright and welcoming, like a star shining to guide you in the right direction on a dark night. I looked around again to see if there were other trees like this one, but this seemed to be the only one.

As I carefully walked in the direction of the tree, about fifty yards away, I took note of the ground, strewn with leaves, small rocks and fragments of decomposing wood. Chirping crickets in the grass grew quiet as I walked by them, and would start their songs again once I walked far enough away from them. I continued watching my steps and surroundings, looking around and turning occasionally, whenever I heard sounds like leaves crackling or twigs snapping, nervous about what might be nearby. As I got closer to the tree's opening, the light coming from within became brighter, yet not so bright that I couldn't look at it.

As I approached, I could see silhouettes of objects in the opening. They seemed like tables, chairs and other large things. I thought to myself, "How could a tree have all this furniture inside of it? Who put these here?"

Now at the entrance, I looked inside. I was somewhat anxious and uncertain about entering the tree, not knowing exactly who or what would be inside. I poked my head in and peeked all around the inside of the tree while standing at the opening. Surprisingly, the light coming from inside the tree was suddenly dimmed, as if in reaction to my arrival. After looking around, and noticing nothing too unusual, given the already abnormal circumstances, I felt it was safe to enter. I don't know why I felt so safe; I just had a good feeling about it.

As I walked in, what I had gathered to be silhouettes of furniture were just what I thought they were. The floor of the tree was hardwood, similar to planks of dark cherry wood—deep red with a rich luster. It struck me as a very fine and expensive flooring that would be found in the opulently decorated home of a wealthy person. There also stood a colorful armless chair and two wooden tables: one rectangular and the other round. The chair was striped in a rainbow of painted colors. It appeared to be made of some type of wood I'd never seen before, carved with beautiful curves and an overall round shape with a high back.

I walked towards it. It was even more beautiful than I originally thought. I touched the chair, more like a throne, following the glossed wood grain with my finger, which was cool and smooth to the touch. I finished admiring the craftsmanship and proceeded to look around the room.

The rectangular table was surrounded by four low stools. On the other hand, the round table, on the opposite side of the room, had three stools and three wooden chairs. There were other pieces of furniture arranged around the room as well. After taking a closer look, the chairs appeared to be a little worn from years of use, but still in very good condition, like someone had been very careful with them.

As I continued to glance around, there was a padlocked chest on the ground by a rocking chair. There were also small shelves laden with books all around the room. I checked out the spines of the books on the shelf closest to me, and picked one up with great care. They seemed to be very old and valuable, with elegant writing in a language I that didn't recognize. I couldn't explain it, but my gut informed me that there was something very special about what was inside of the books, although I couldn't read them.

The walls of the room were also adorned with magnificent paintings of landscapes with mountains, forests and castles. One of these paintings depicted a city which didn't match the tone of the other pictures. This city and the surrounding streets looked vaguely familiar....

Suddenly, before I could look closer, I stopped, a bit alarmed. "Did I hear something...?"

There was a low, windy, breathing sound coming from underneath one of the doors where bright light seemed to be emanating from. I first turned around to look outside the tree opening, but saw nothing outside but leaves blowing in the wind.

As I approached the door where the breathing was coming from, the light became brighter, as if to beckon me. The sound frightened me a little, but I knew I had to investigate.

The door was made of the same wood that the tree was made of, kind of pine-like, which was a lighter color than the dark cherry-like flooring and furniture. The door was in good shape like the rest of the woodwork in the room. The knob, which was round, had a golden keyhole underneath, covered with scratches from being clumsily nicked by keys for years.

I slowly grabbed the handle, not sure of what would happen, listening, and turned the handle clockwise to open the door. It began to open, but then felt like it was stuck. I didn't want to be too forceful because I was afraid to make any noise, for fear that it would alarm whoever was breathing inside the room. I put my shoulder into it carefully and the door budged open.

After opening the door a crack, I noticed that in the bright room were a number of other petite bookcases filled with old tomes. I stepped into the room and saw two huge wooden doors to my left. The doors were close to each other, one on the right and one on the left of a long table in the middle of the room. The bright light that had originally attracted me to this tree came from a hidden object in the corner.

The object was covered with a brown woolen blanket. It seemed to have fallen on top, hiding the light. Or maybe someone had placed it there. I walked towards the covered light, and again I heard the eerie breathing sound coming from one of the doors. The door on the left was slightly cracked open while the door closest to me was fully closed.

I approached the door that was slightly ajar to peek into the adjoining room. From what I could see through the crack inside, it was very dark. Standing with my face pressed up against the doorframe, I then heard a low, raspy, male voice say, "Lorenz—you may enter the room."

Startled, I immediately jumped and looked at the slightly opened door. Frightened, I took a couple of steps back and bumped into one of the benches next to the long table, nearly knocking over the potted plants and decorative vases precariously arranged on the arm rests. I stood there for a moment, staring into the narrow sliver of blackness. Nothing happened.

Gathering up my courage, I decided to listen to the voice and enter. I walked to the cracked door and opened it all the way. Sensing my presence again, the voice continued. He spoke clearly and with authority.

"Welcome to my world. I've observed you for a while now and know of your troubles. I've also seen what lies ahead for you. If you are willing, my world can help make things better for you in yours."

I stood there, stunned and listening to this voice talk to me in the darkness. I thought about my bigger adult body and the strange way in how I had gotten here as he spoke. I didn't know who was talking to me, but he seemed to mean well.

"When you go between our two realms, you will be different in some ways, as you can clearly see. As in your world, there is good and evil in this land and you must choose to use your newfound strength in the right way."

As the voice continued, I listened, bewildered by the things he was telling me, and still wondering what was going on. I had a million burning questions, but dared not interrupt him. The voice thankfully answered some of the big questions that were bouncing around in my head in the next part of his lecture.

"You were chosen for a number of reasons; one reason in particular is your heart. From what I saw in your future, it seemed to me that you would accept my gift. You are still young and have much to learn, and have much potential. You may use this land to travel, meet others, and learn new skills from your experiences. Remember that only the knowledge that you gain in my world can help you in yours, as material possessions you obtain here will always here remain."

I touched my pocket as the voice paused for a brief moment, thinking of the mysterious object that had taken me here. Again, as if noticing my thoughts, the voice kept speaking.

"The gem you found will provide entry into this realm. As you develop your abilities, you may learn to enter this world with other tools as well. The gem can only be used by you as its appearance and power in the hands of anyone else will change. Also, when you enter my world, no one will know that your consciousness has traveled here, as your body stays in your home world living out its normal life as you would normally, in a split form of consciousness, though time passes by at a faster rate than it does here."

The voice paused for another moment. This time, I took the opportunity to finally ask in a timid voice, "Who are you?"

"I am the Creator," the voice replied. "I am the one who starts and the one who finishes. I have been and always will be. You will never see me as I am, as I am both everywhere and nowhere."

I tried to fit in another question, but he quickly cut me short.

"The answers to all of your questions will be provided as you journey in my world. No more questions for now."

I stood in shock, not knowing what to say or think, yet I felt safe in this room with the disembodied voice, as funny as that sounded. I just knew that I would be okay here. I thought to myself things like: What did I do for this to happen to me of all people? What if I said no? What was next?

Finally, I asked aloud, "...What do I have to do now?"

The voice's reply was, "Listen, pay attention and follow directions. You will be given all the tools needed to succeed."

I nodded my head, acknowledging that I understood.

He continued. "In this world, you shall be called by the name of Lorenz. Your origin will be the region of NotingShaw in the land of StaE. Your body is now the equivalent of one of twenty-one years of age. Your only concerns for now should be to take care of yourself and your instructions. You will meet and interact with many beings of different races, and also many creatures, beasts and others animals similar to those in your world. You must make choices about how they will assist or hinder you from reaching your goals."

The Creator took a slow breath and sounded like he was finishing up his speech. "It is now time for you to return to your world. When the time is right for you to come back here, the gem will give you a sign. When you next reenter this land, return to this place. I will provide you with all that you need to help you achieve your goals and complete the tasks that lay before you." Finally, the room became silent.

I knew that it was time to leave. As I turned around, leaving the room where the Creator's voice came from, everything I looked at was still the same. As I walked out of the enormous hollow tree, I grinned, imagining myself as a great leader with super powers and special abilities.

I headed back to the general location that I remembered landing in. I knew when I had reached the right spot, since I immediately began to feel that familiar, uncomfortable tingling in my stomach. I closed my eyes to try to relax myself and waited for a while for the disorientation to pass. When I peeked a bit through one careful eye, I found myself in the exact place where I was before the crazy forest adventure!

I was at the stairs in the front of the basement backdoor, amongst mountains of dented cardboard boxes smelling of damp mold and mildew. After confirming my location, I checked my clothing. Everything was normal. I breathed a sigh of relief. I was back to wearing my usual, everyday clothes: black and white tennis shoes, blue jeans and my favorite blue and white striped polo shirt.

CHAPTER TWO

Once I had settled down, I found that it was disappointing to hear the angry voices of my relatives above me again. Wanting to return to the Creator's magical world, I reached for the small pyramid-shaped gem which was still in the palm of my hand. I attempted to twist the top to see if I could go back. Sadly, nothing happened. I placed the gem within my right pants pocket with a disappointed sigh.

Not really wanting to go back in the house, I headed towards the back iron gate. I opened the gate, lifting the rusty latch and pushing it open. I wanted to head back to the place that I had picked up the magical gem, to look more closely at the spot to see if there were any other clues around.

There was nothing else special or shining here but pieces of green glass from a broken beer bottle. I kept walking. I was moving, but I had no destination. I couldn't help but think about having just travelled to another world. I couldn't remember every detail, but I had such vivid images in my mind. It was almost like a dream, except I knew that it couldn't be, since the weird artifact lay in my pocket as proof.

I wasn't sure of what time of the day it was. "Is it different from when I left?" I wondered. It was still hot and humid. I would learn that it was still the same Sunday in late September, though several hours later, even though I had only been in the other world for a few minutes.

I heard the sounds of kids playing as I wandered aimlessly around and around, back and forth, thinking. Suddenly, the sound of my aunt's voice rang out loudly, calling my name. Not wanting to get into trouble, I started sprinting out of the alley, turning left onto the sidewalk. Within moments, I was running up the front steps of the house. I saw some kids with whom I normally played with zooming around playing tag. I ran past them, up the stairs onto the gray painted front porch of the house and burst inside, replying to my aunt.

She shouted at me with a dirty look, "Where have you been!? I've been calling you for ten whole minutes! Didn't you hear me, Lorenzo?"

I knew she was exaggerating. It hadn't even been ten seconds. "I was out playing, Aunt Georgia," I replied. "I'm sorry."

Georgia huffed and then said sternly, "Next time I call you, you better answer me, boy! Go back outside, but only out front until I call you for dinner!" She glared at me and then at the ground by my feet. "And don't you dare track any dirt in the house or you'll be vacuuming tonight!"

"Yes ma'am." I nodded to her and went back outside, thoughts still spinning over the fantastical happenings of just a half hour ago. After pushing open the screen door, I ran down the stairs and onto the sidewalk, meeting the other kids. When I reached the sidewalk, the other children were still busily playing tag. I asked them, "Hey, can I join in?"

"Yeah, but you're it, Lorenzo!" One boy playfully ran up and tagged me "it," as he named this prerequisite. I happily obliged.

I let the worries and thoughts slip out of mind for a small while, just having fun, playing with my friends. We chased each other around until the clock struck seven o'clock and it was dinnertime.

Right on schedule, Georgia called out in her booming voice, "Lorenzo, come inside for dinner!"

Some of the kids groaned as I headed back home. Waving good-bye, I told them, "I have to go inside now, guys. See you later."

By this time, the sun was starting to go down. I ran up the stairs, towards the front door, but when I reached the porch, my aunt stopped me by standing in the way. "Have you seen Darius?" she asked, tapping my fingers against her arm impatiently.

"No, I was just on the corner—" I started to reply.

"Just get in the house!" Georgia snapped, taking out her frustration of my brother's whereabouts on me. Honestly, he was probably at a neighbor's house, playing violent video games or watching R rated movies. My aunt stood there, just calling for Darius, so that I had to maneuver around her round frame to get inside.

We had meatloaf with mashed potatoes and steamed broccoli that night. My brother finally came back home by the time we were all almost done eating. I had eaten my share quickly and put my dishes into the sink because I wanted to hurry to the privacy of my room.

As I started up the stairs, my aunt asked me suspiciously, "Where are you going?" She was prying because I was heading upstairs much sooner than usual.

"I'm going to take my bath and get ready for bed early today," I replied. "I feel kind of tired."

A bit surprised, she blurted out with emphasis, "Good!" As far as she was concerned, it was all the less that she had to see of me for the rest of the day.

I climbed the carpeted stairs to the bathroom after gathering my blue and green striped pajamas, my bath towel and a fresh wash cloth. I was afraid that someone might find the gem while I was washing up, so I decided it would be best to leave it in my pocket until I got into the bathroom. There, I would hide the gem in my pajamas as I went back down to my room.

The bathroom walls were covered in ceramic green tiles with matching grout, which Georgia made me scrub clean every week. I prepared for bed, which included brushing my teeth until they were clean and minty fresh and then began to draw a bath. It was especially refreshing during the summer, to cool down and wash off all of the day's sweat.

I stopped the bathtub drain, turned on the tap and let the water run to warm up and fill the tub. I took out the gem and looked at it in amazement, murmuring to it quietly, "Where did you come from...? How did you get here?"

While I was distracted thinking about the gem, I had forgotten that someone might be able to come into the bathroom and see it. I immediately made sure that the door was securely locked. Nervous, I quickly placed it into my pajama pants pocket for safe-keeping.

I then heard my aunt yell from downstairs, "That's enough water, Lorenz! Stop wasting the water!"

She kept grumbling loudly afterwards, probably about how I never thought about all the utility bills she had to pay. Not wanting her to come upstairs to complain, I promptly turned off the water, even though the tub wasn't yet full or very hot.

Fifteen minutes had passed and I finished taking my bath. After drying off and feeling squeaky clean, I put on my pajamas with the gem securely in place and went back downstairs to bed.

Unlike everyone else's room, my bedroom was located on the first floor, next to the kitchen, such that it was the smallest and noisiest room. I could hear everything my family did in the kitchen or living room from in there.

After I got under the covers, I pat my pocket gently, ensuring the gem was still there. In my twin size bed, I laid there, thinking about the gem and its strange powers. Thoughts of it and memories of the day permeated my mind. I tried to remember in detail the many things that happened throughout the day. I was excited to think about what might come next.

After I finished my homework, I passed the next few hours, pondering and pacing around nervously. It gradually became silent enough in the house to know that no one was walking around the first floor anymore. I took the gem from out of my pocket while hiding under the covers. I placed it in the safest place I could think of outside my pocket: under my pillow, within the pillowcase.

Several times during the night, I woke up thinking about the gem, worrying if it had been stolen or if it was all just a dream, and then I'd slide my hand under the pillow to make sure it was still there. It always was.

The next morning when I awoke, the first thing I did was dress and hide the artifact in my jeans. Before I had too much time to dwell on anything, the delicious smell of a pancake breakfast and my hungry stomach growling interrupted any thoughts of magical adventures. The excitement of the past day had really worked up an appetite!

After eating, I promptly left the house by myself. As usual, my brother was still lingering around the house, taking his time eating and getting ready. He'd be late for school again, at this rate, even though school was only about a few blocks away.

It was just north up the street, over the crosswalk at the corner of 6th and F. This morning, my thoughts were on what was in my blue jeans pocket. I couldn't wait to get somewhere private to look at the mysterious object again. Wanting to see it, my pace quickened, needing to find a safe place to take it out. Everywhere I looked, I saw moms out to buy groceries, or kids walking to school in groups with their friends.

As I got closer to the school, I couldn't help but want to take a quick glance, despite not having a safe place to hide. I looked to my right and left after I turned a nearby corner with fewer people walking around. They were far away enough though that I decided they shouldn't notice anything out of the ordinary. I had a few seconds.

Anxious, I reached into my pocket and pulled the gem out. Boy, the excitement I felt! I could've jumped up and down a thousand times.

It brought back memories of the tree in that amazing forest. "I want to go back!" I wished to it in a hushed voice.

As I held it in my hands, I noticed a striking design at the bottom. One side had a symbol engraved in it shaped almost like an animal. What was it? I could make out that it had a muzzle with fangs and had a long tail and big eyes. I started to twist at the top of the gem when I heard something other than cars passing by.

I immediately looked up and there were a couple of kids with their parents only a few feet away. I quickly placed it back into my pocket. "I better get to school or I'll be late, and then I'll be in big trouble with Georgia." I warned myself.

When I arrived at school, everything there was as usual aside from the swirling thoughts in my mind. I wanted to be in the other world—not this run-down excuse of an elementary school infested with moronic bullies. A wadded up paper ball flew and bounced off my desk, rolling by my foot and there was snickering from behind me. I rolled my eyes and kept working on my math worksheets. The teacher was oblivious, but it didn't matter. I couldn't count on anyone here, as even the school faculty shrugged off the harassment they saw every day. All the teachers and staff seemed to be afflicted with a numb apathy and justified themselves in not helping kids like me with their problems by telling themselves that there were bigger issues to spend their time worrying about.

Even though I wasn't a violent person myself, I sometimes wished I that I was bigger and able to open up a can of "whoop ass" on the malicious students that picked on me. Still, I was in 6th grade now and I just needed to get through one more year. Then I could have a fresh start somewhere else.

During lunchtime today at school, while I was minding my own business, eating one of those questionable mini burgers that they serve to students, a yell echoed throughout the cafeteria. I was so used to the incessant shouting that I didn't even look up. An apple came soaring at me along with that cry though, and pegged me square in the shoulder, then fell into my lunch tray, scattering my fries all over the place. I stopped to look for the idiot who threw the nasty, half-eaten apple core at me. It had come from somewhere across the room.

With disgust, I glanced across the cafeteria, but it was impossible to tell who it was in the crowd of eating students. I lost my appetite and didn't finish my meal. I just grabbed my lunch tray hastily and put it away. I was too frustrated and didn't want to stay to be a target for another piece of fruit, or something worse. I left the lunchroom and headed outside to try to enjoy the rest of my free time.

As soon as I entered the playground, the sounds of laughter, chatter and happy screams encouraged me to run for the swings at the far end of the playground. Halfway from the school building and the jungle gym though, I thought I felt something move in my pocket. It was the gem shaking. Anxious and excited, I ran past the playground to an area on the school grounds where no other students were hanging around.

I found a spot to hide at the corner of an old portable classroom nearby. There, I sat with my back propped up against side of the building. After making sure that no one was nearby or watching me, I took the gem from out of my pocket. As I looked at the pyramidal artifact, the deep purple and gold surface sparkled and glinted, partly from the sunlight and partly through a power of its own.

I could feel my heart fill with excitement and my expression showed likewise. While I looked at the gem and its incredible light, out of nowhere, I heard the talking voices of two 4th grade schoolmates—a boy and girl. They were running right towards me!

I was startled and immediately jammed the thing back into the pocket of my jeans. I didn't manage to hide it in time, but the two just ran right past me. They were so engaged with each other, laughing and bantering that I don't think they even realized I was there.

After looking again to see if anyone else was coming, I started to slowly reach into my pocket to remove the gem, when all of a sudden, my pocket started moving again on its own. I jumped a little in surprise from the sudden sensation. When I pulled out the gem this time, it was jiggling excitedly around in my palm, as if desperately trying to get my attention. I then remembered what the voice had said to me yesterday. The gem would let me know when I needed to return.

Without hesitation, I quickly twisted the top until I felt it click. Again, I felt the tingling in my stomach. I was moving up and down, around and around. I had no idea what direction I was moving in; it was like I was falling in every direction at once. When the vertigo subsided and it seemed that I was slowing down, and the lush green canopy of the forest faded into view, I made an attempt to try and land on my two feet in the new world.

CHAPTER THREE

With my eyes open, I landed in the same spot, but on my feet this time. Instead of falling on my butt, I fell onto my knees from the hard sudden impact with the ground. I immediately jumped up, looked around and everything seemed the same. The same birds and crickets called and the same tall grass rubbed their crystalline dew on my knees. As I headed to the hollow tree in a brisk jog, I checked my clothing. They were the familiar leather and copper fatigues.

I entered the big tree opening, briefly noting that everything was the like the first time I'd entered. I headed to the door that I had visited before, where the voice had started speaking to me. Upon reaching the door, I turned the knob and opened it. I stood in the door's entrance and waited.

Silence permeated the room. I stood there blankly for a few moments, waiting for something to happen. Just when I thought that maybe he wasn't there, without notice, the voice from before started to speak loud and clear, startling me.

"Welcome, Lorenz." The voice was still low and raspy, but his loud voice boomed in my ears.

"Hello," I said back to him in greeting. I didn't know where to focus as I spoke to the voice, so I just stared at the nicely carved chair I had admired the last time, as if some invisible being were sitting there.

The Creator continued. "You got here quickly this time. Excellent."

I didn't reply, waiting for what was next.

"I need you to make your first choice. In this room on your right, you will find three black leather sacks lined up along the wall. You will find within one of the sacks that you choose, items that will be useful for you in challenging situations. They will grant you knowledge that you need and protection from grave danger. Only touch the sack that you are certain to choose. The first one you touch will be yours."

I was quite curious and anxious after hearing what the Creator said. I entered the room after he finished giving instructions, but the room was totally dark. I around looked for some sign of the Creator, wanting to get a glimpse of who I'd been talking to, yet found no one.

As he mentioned, to my right were the items he had said were in the room. I stepped further in, looking and feeling around the dark room, trying to get a sense of my surroundings, but being careful not to touch anything that seemed sack-like. The gem began to glow within my pocket on its own, lighting the place up so that I could see.

I lifted the gem and guided it around the room like a flashlight. Looking around, my eyes fell upon the three black leather bags the Creator was talking about. I took mental note of the furniture in the room along with the sacks. There was a long table that resembled a dining table and two stools made of a dark wood on either end. On the table also was a place setting for two to sit, but no plates, forks, or knives. A clay pitcher sat lonely on the tabletop.

What was this room for? Maybe it was a back-up dining room, or an office space, I imagined. Where was the source of that voice? Though I searched and wondered, I was unable to identify anything that would tell me where he was speaking from.

The voice instantly interrupted my efforts by snapping in an impatient tone, "Stop wasting time!"

Fearful that I might make the voice upset, I decided to focus on the leather bags as he had commanded. I stood in the middle of the room, examining the sacks. They reminded me of the times I did my family's laundry. I would fill up a big pillowcase full of clothes and take them to the local Laundromat since we didn't own a personal washing machine or dryer.

I sized each bag up. They were all big, but the bag on the left seemed less full than the one in the middle. On the other hand, the one on the right seemed slightly taller than the one in the middle. I looked at each sack again trying to find a reason to take one over the other. I leaned in to get a closer look, lowering the gem, still glowing; I hoped that with its bright light, I could see within the sacks. Careful not to touch any of the bags, even this close, I could see no difference in them other than what I had already noticed. Finally, I felt drawn to the middle one.

I reached out my left hand to grab the bag, holding the gem in my right. I grabbed the top of the middle black sack, picked it up and headed towards the door, which was still open. As I headed into the other room, I heard the voice say, "Good choice. I knew you would choose wisely."

I instinctively whirled around to look behind me, lifting up the gem to provide light. I glanced around briefly, finding nothing. This truly puzzled me. How was it that the voice was coming from this room and the other room? Maybe there were little speakers hidden everywhere, or the person really was invisible? I also wondered if the voice really knew that I was going to choose the bag that I chose and how it could know such a thing. Could it really tell the future, like it had suggested yesterday? I lowered the gem, turned around and started back out of the room.

The Creator then instructed me to sit in the chair in the middle of the room. I did as I was told.

The chair was facing the bookshelf opposite the entrance of the tree. While sitting, I placed my leather bag down and put the gem back into my pocket. I was somewhat surprised at how comfortable the chair was despite being made of hard wood. The Creator instructed me to look into the sack I chose, so I began rummaging through it.

The first item I removed seemed to be a bladed weapon of some sort. Living in the inner city, I had never seen one of these aside from on TV. For all intents and purposes, it was a big, shiny sword.

What would I need this for? The sword was about the length of my entire arm. The grip fit my hand perfectly, like it was custom-made for me. Further down the hilt, towards the blade, was a rounded cross guard. The blade was silver with pressed grooves following the edges, elevating the center of the blade stylishly into a broad central ridge. I closely examined and felt the blade. Even though it was fairly plain, the blade seemed solid and was extremely sharp to the touch. I got up out of the chair and started testing its weight in my hand. I found it to be light-weight and easy to wield, as if I had taken lessons before!

"How is this possible?" I stammered. I didn't remember ever doing this, even when playing or roughhousing with other kids. The closest I had ever come to wielding a sword was watching a fight scene between cartoon knights or pirates on television! As soon as I was about to open my mouth to ask further, my gut told me that now was not the time. Frankly, it was just cool that I knew how to swing a sword around without killing myself.

My attention went away from the sword and back to the bag. I laid the blade down next to the chair carefully. "What else is in this sack?"

I reached into the big bag with my right hand and pulled out something that was all rolled up. It felt like old, tough paper, like parchment. It was tattered and appeared to be white originally, but was now yellowed and smudged with dirt. The paper was in some kind of translucent protective wrapping. The outside of the wrap felt rough like sandpaper. I looked at it closely trying to figure out how to get the parchment roll out of the wrap and found the dividing section where I could begin to separate it.

I could see lines and shapes scrawled onto the yellow parchment. The lines looked kind of like roads. There were shaded areas that vaguely resembled moun-tain tops or rivers. There were also words written in recognizable letters that seemed like they could be the names of places, maybe towns and cities or land-marks. The writing was clearly legible and written in a flowing black ink.

I stretched out the parchment to look at the entire roll. Though it was clearly some sort of map, what city or town or landmark I was by, I didn't know. There was no way I could tell where I was.

The voice asked me, "What do you think you are holding?"

I could hear the voice so clearly, like he was standing right next to me. With-out looking up this time, keeping a good hold of the parchment, which wanted to roll back up from being wrapped up for so long, I replied to him. "It's a map."

The voice grunted in approval and continued to explain, "Yes. This map will help guide you through my world. There are many roads, leading through many mountains, valleys, plains, forests, caves, towns and cities, and much more."

My eyes glided along the map's features as he kept explaining.

"It will help guide you on your journey, and will get you to the places you need to go. You must, however, learn how to use the map in order for it to assist you. Should you ever become lost in your way, this map can put you back on the right path. You must learn on your own how to use this which I have given you."

Knowing that I was being overwhelmed by all the things that he was giving me and telling me, the Creator tried to calm my thoughts by saying, "Lorenz, you will have questions, but understand that answers to those questions will eventually come. You must have patience. You will find the answers not when you want them, but at a time that you need them."

I didn't respond.. It seemed I was on a "need to know" basis.

I looked at the map again. I didn't recognize any of the names of the places on the map at all. How would I navigate myself to these distant places? The only traveling I ever did was from inside a car with my mom, and I wasn't even the one driving! How I was going to traverse a huge landscape like this was going to be an interesting challenge. I rolled the map back up gently and set it aside, near the sword.

I stretched open the top of the bag again, reaching in and grabbing hold of something else rough to the touch and pulled out what looked like a dark rectangular leather object. This flat object was folded up and about as long as my arm. I saw no markings or symbols on it, unlike the map. As I unfolded it, I noticed that it was not rectangular, but in the shape of a square with a tapering point on the bottom. On the back of it in the middle was a handle that I could slip the four of my hand fingers under, with my thumb around the other side. I did so, to test it out.

Immediately, this item transformed from pliable leather to a very hard material, like metal, except it wasn't any heavier! I took my hand out and tucked the handle away against the back and it transformed to a soft, foldable textile again.

I tried it one more time. This time, I put the object near my body, bringing it to my chest. It stretched out and molded itself to cover my entire torso. It was like having a protective hard shell that somehow allowed me complete range of movement by following every movement of my body like a second skin. I could still twist and bend just fine. Nothing like this could possibly exist.

"This is some kind of shield?" I asked in amazement.

The voice answered me. "This is a treasure that will protect you when you are in physical danger. It is an excellent defense, but beware, as there are some things from which even this item cannot guard you."

What would I face that would require me to have this huge sword and crazy magic shield? Fear began to grow inside me along with the curiosity. What in the world was in store for me? It was starting to sound pretty dangerous.

I reached into the sack once again. It seemed pretty empty, but when I shook it a little, it made a clinking noise inside. I reached into the bag and fumbled my hand around thoroughly. The last item I felt was small. I pulled it out.

It was a small dark velvety pouch filled with something hard. At the top was an opening with a drawstring. The contents of this little pouch were heavy and felt like metal. I opened it and poured them out into my hand. The items were silvery, square and very thin. There were about ten of them. There were no designs on them, but the edges were adorned with really small ridges all the way around them, like a quarter. I didn't know what they were, but I made a guess to myself that they might be a form of currency here.

"Maybe I use this as money." I put the strange-looking square coins back into the small pouch and looked one last time at everything and then put all of the items back into the black sack. The sword, the map and the shield were once again neatly tucked away along with the money pouch.

I leaned back against the chair to think. In my head, I went through all of the items I acquired. A little bit more anxiety quickened my heart rate when I again thought to myself why I would need this kind of heavy duty protection.

In my world, I hadn't really learned how to fight. I had been in only a few fights, and those hadn't turned out so well, plus I'd been grounded for weeks for them. I suddenly imagined that the sword or shield would be really awesome to take back to my home world. I could show them off to my friends and I'd have loved to see a bully try to sock me in the stomach while I was wearing the armored skin. Then I remembered what the voice had said; I couldn't take items away from this world, only knowledge.

This series of thoughts was interrupted by the voice calling me from a distance. He'd said my name twice before I realized it. I looked up.

"Lorenz, it is important to listen to what I am about to tell you. I would like for you to travel to the town of 'Wortheast.' There, in that town you will find a man who will help you. He will give you things that will help you very greatly on your journeys. You now have everything you need to begin. While traveling on your quest, you will have the opportunity to gather other tools that will help you. Make sure that you pay attention to your surroundings and follow directions. Adhere to these points and you will thrive."

The locked chest in the room that I had noticed last time suddenly shook and clanked, the padlock falling right off onto the floor.

"In the chest in front of you, go and get food for your journey. Take only what you need."

I waited until I thought the voice was finished. When it was clear that he was not going to say any more for now, I lifted myself out of the chair, grabbed my bag and headed towards the chest as the voice instructed.

I opened the top of the chest, resting the round hinged cover against the wall behind it gently. I looked inside to find a variety of foods. There were loaves of fragrant rye bread, shiny red apples, citrus fruits, whole carrots, and bags of various nuts and other things.

There were also numerous bottles and flasks wrapped in cloth. I started picking some of the food items and bottles of water, placing them carefully in my sack with the other things. I remembered what the voice had told me—not to take more than I would need.

It was hard to choose how much was what I needed since I had never done something like this before, but I tried to imagine what I would need if I went camping with my mom for the weekend, so I took an amount that I thought might keep me full for a few days.

After gathering enough food, the voice then said, "Listen carefully, Lorenz. You are to head to the region of Waeaginia to find someone. There, in the foot of the mountains, off the main road you will find whom you seek. There will be significant obstacles and many challenges along the way, as well as people that may help or hinder you. Remember the things that I told you to do and you will always succeed."

After that last statement, there was complete silence. It was clear that the voice was done speaking to me.

Almost ready, I realized I needed to look at the map and figure out where to go. I reached in and pulled out the map and oriented it appropriately. I searched for

Waeaginia, the region the voice was talking about, dragging my fingertip gently over the parchment surface, reading the names. I found it after a few seconds. It was in a larger area named Waealand. In this region, I found the town Wortheast. Where was I right now, though?

At home, I had learned how to interpret maps early on as a kid, while riding with my mother on long road trips, but that didn't seem to help much now. I looked closer at the map, staring very pointedly at the labels, unsure of how I was going to know which way to go.

I thought about the transforming shield. Could this map change itself too? Just as I thought that, only inches away from the destination of Wortheast, appeared a clear black dot. This dot hovered over a new image that had extensions or branches... like maybe a big tree! I wondered if the black circular dot showed my current location in the tree hollow. If that was true, then following the map wouldn't be too difficult. From the dot, I saw a road that led towards the top of the map, presumably the equivalent of north.

It was time. "Well, I better go and get started." I felt a sense of excitement and anxiety, not knowing what I was going to face.

I decided to fold up the map and put it into my pocket, so I would have quick and easy access to it. I then looked at the sack, trying to figure out a way to carry everything and still be comfortable. Carrying it in my arms would be heavy and straining. Conveniently, I found a better way to do it. There were two hidden straps that I could pull out to elongate and put my arms through, like a backpack.

I put on my trusty new "backpack" and headed to the entrance of the tree. When I got to the opening, I looked both ways and then looked down at the map to determine which direction to go. Then, I was off.

CHAPTER FOUR

L eaving the tree's entrance, I turned left, into ever more trees. As I walked north through the grove, I observed everything around me including the sounds of beautifully singing birds. All around me were huge, amazing trees with oversized round trunks. The ridged brown branches all looked very strong. Hanging from the branches were large green and brown leaves. Damp moss, fringed lichens, and rainbows of bracket fungus decorated the trunks' bark. The singing birds of many species and many plumages and colors flitted around the branches and clung to the tree trunks with their clawed feet as they searched for food.

As I walked by the trees, I touched the huge trunks and hanging foliage within my reach. The trunks felt rough and dusty. I heard the wind rustling the leaves on the ground and on the branches. The weather was cool and refreshing—not hot and smoggy like at home. The urban odors of cigarette smoke, partially combusted gasoline and dumpsters were nowhere to be found here. It was just the soft smells of moist dirt, waving grass and pine-scented trees.

As I continued to walk, I looked down and it seemed that a small path was becoming more apparent. The dirt was more trodden and packed down. I could see where others had come this way in the past and blazed this trail, cutting down shrubs and hacking away branches that were in the way.

I continued down the path looking right and left, catching glimpses of flitting insects and birds. I had walked about a mile when I noticed that the trees seemed to be coming to an end. I was beginning to approach a real road, so I stopped to take in the view ahead of me. When I looked back to see the hollow tree where the voice was, I noticed it was strangely gone.

"Did I already walk that far?"

Maybe I was too far from the tree to see it or maybe it had disappeared. I was unsure, but kept on forging ahead. I had a task I had to complete.

Ahead in the distance appeared what seemed like hills or mountains. They were really lovely. The knolls were covered with light green grass and dotted with wildflowers. Embedded in the ground were strangely-shaped rock formations scattered randomly throughout the swaying grassy meadows. My heart seemed to soar as I observed this incredible sight.

Such breath-taking beauty caused me to stop for a minute right there, at the edge of the forest. I bent down to touch the grass and feel the texture. The green blades were smooth and soft, easily bowing under my gentlest touch; it was like touching downy feathers. The groups of rocks were like those I remembered from stone quarries on TV: big, blocky and chiseled-looking, sitting in piles.

Then all of a sudden, CRASH!

I jumped, startled by the sound of rocks tumbling down the hillside together. I looked towards the top of one of the hills. There was something looking down in my direction, standing at the peak. Whatever it was, it matched the color of the landscape in such a way that it camouflaged with its surroundings very well.

This creature stood on four legs and had thick green matted fur and branching horns stretching across its head from left to right. It sort of resembled the antlers of a reindeer except minus the Santa Claus.

The animal looked like it was chewing big mouthfuls of grass, ripping it from the ground with its teeth. It glanced down in my direction and after grabbing another mouthful, continued chewing, ignoring me. It was only one that I saw, but I wondered if there were more that I wasn't noticing.

I looked to the left and saw other creatures, none of which I recognized. There were smaller animals coming out of burrows in the ground. They looked like large rats, with exaggeratedly long snouts, big beady eyes and dark fuzzy fur. There were several of them walking in a group. They might be a family. Despite the interesting fauna all around me, I didn't have the luxury to sit around all day watching them. It was time to move on, so I kept walking north.

While moving forward, I began to hear unusual sounds like the chattering of wild animals. Instead of being nervous about it, I tried to envision what the sources of the sounds were. The chattering noise reminded me of monkeys; I wondered what monkeys here might look like. My pace was slow and steady, enabling me to save my energy while appreciating all that was around me.

The amount of leaves and grass on the road eventually diminished as the road bed transitioned to a more rocky consistency. Luckily, my tough boots protected my feet, no matter how sharp the rocks were. As I went on, the mountain range peeking in the distance gradually became higher and wider, hour after hour. Finally, I realized the sun's—actually, the two suns' position in the sky had changed significantly. They had not only moved to the left, but it was much larger, almost double in size and more oval in shape. I couldn't even begin to imagine what sort of star or planetary orbit would cause a weird visual effect like that.

With the sun shining on me, I felt the warmth beaming down on my face. I was sweaty and hot from all the walking, carrying the heavy backpack, but the sunlight still felt good on my skin. It was invigorating, even. I imagined this must be kind of how Superman felt in sunlight, recharging his strength and powers. I refocused on the task at hand, shaking away the silly ideas, and observing what was around me while heading north to my destination.

Occasionally, I would kneel down to feel the earth around me. There was gravelly soil bearing small trees that were orange and red in color with little branches and very thin round leaves. The outer edges, midribs and veins of the leaves were orange while the leaf bodies themselves were red. I wondered if that was their summer or fall color or if they just always looked like that.

As I approached a turn in the road, the road began to rise as it climbed a hill. The sides of the increasingly taller hills were still green, but the tops seemed higher and the slopes steeper. On the left, down the road was a jutting mountain that seemed very high. The mountain had a mixture of scraggly shrubbery and big, red rocks in the higher elevations. To the right finally were some buildings. There were people here! The buildings looked like rounded square cabins made of reddish brown logs painted with orange stripes.

Behind these buildings, there were more trees like the ones in the forest I had left. "Boy, these buildings sure are different," I muttered quietly to myself.

I wondered who might live in the structures and if they would be friendly. There were at least eight of these buildings that I could see. Some were by the road and others were further from the road, amongst the trees. While still far away, I decide to hide behind a large boulder. From what I could see, there were herds of snowy white goats grazing and numerous people out walking around and talking, going about their daily business. They looked human and there were both adults and children present.

I was really scared and excited at the same time as I watched them, crouching and unseen. I had to do something though. I couldn't just keep sitting there, so I continued warily towards the settlement, trying to play it cool.

I was looking forward to talking with someone, but I didn't know what might happen if I did. As I approached, the people didn't seem to stop what they were doing even though they looked in my direction and could clearly see me. They minded their own business, just talking, walking, and going in and out of the buildings. Some of them were very tall and heavyset, some were short and stocky, and still others were in between.

I decided that I better pull out the map to get another look at where I was and where I needed to go. I looked and found with the black dot that I was right on track. The buildings were on the map and where I had to go was down the road a ways, near the really tall mountain range. I was a little curious about this settlement though.

There was a building immediately to my right. No one was in front of this square building, so I decided that maybe I ought to go in and see what was inside. I headed towards the front door. On the left side of the door was a sign hanging on the wall reading "Ashawa."

There were a couple of steps to climb before reaching the approximately eight foot door. As I approached, reaching out my hand to open it, the door was pulled back away from me, which surprised me. A man as tall as I was had swung it open and begun to walk out. He had long red hair with bangs covering his large green eyes, and he was wearing similar clothes to mine. Small knives and daggers matted with dried blood and fur hung on the sides of his leather trousers. Maybe a hunter. I moved to the side to allow him to pass. The man simply left the door open without a second thought, as if to allow me to go inside, so I held the door open and took one step in.

Inside, I saw a large room with various items, people and animals, all with different shapes and sizes. This room was large and rectangular and filled with tables and shelves. There was a counter with a couple of people behind it, cooking, cleaning and chatting. Behind them were shelves stocked with food, clothing, bottles and other things. The goods were clearly items on display for being sold.

There were tables, round or square in shape, made of wood of different hues. Fresh candles sat on the tables, ready to cast their warm glow for whoever would light them. A few of the tables already had people dining at them.

This place looked like some kind of bar or restaurant with a convenience store in the back. I was still at the front door with it slightly opened, feeling out of place. Those behind the counter stared at me, adding to my awkward feeling. I realized then that maybe I should come in and close the door.

I closed the entrance and slowly walked in, trying to look as casual and normal as possible. Those behind the counter then went back to what they were doing before. As I walked in, the others didn't take special notice of me. I was a bit surprised that they didn't seem to care that a complete stranger had just walked into the room, but I wasn't going to complain. Maybe they got a lot of travelers and were used to it. I relaxed a little and took a look around.

The food and the bottles behind the counter, which were arranged in no special order, intrigued me. The smell of roasted meat was heavy in the air, but I wasn't too hungry. I was just really thirsty from all the walking. I had some water in my bag, but I thought maybe I should take the opportunity in soaking in some of the culture here while I had the chance.

The bottles on display had various colored fluids in them. I wondered what they were for. Were they magical potions, special medicines, or simply refreshing beverages? I looked around the room to see what bottles were being drunk by those eating at the dining tables. I found that most people were drinking the frothy gold liquid. It looked like beer. I decided that I would try to buy something to drink here too, since I was parched from the trek.

I went up to the counter. A man, tall and brawny in build, came to serve me. He was large, with thick limbs made of bulging muscle. His head was shaved bald; you could even see a small scabbed cut where he had apparently gotten nicked by his shaving razor. His beady eyes were small and brown in color, under heavy red eyebrows which matched his rich ruddy beard.

When I timidly approached the counter, the huge man grunted out to me, "What can I get for you?"

I was at first surprised to hear him speak in English, but then again, that disembodied voice of the Creator also spoke to me in English. Maybe English was a major language of this land, or maybe we could just magically understand each other. I didn't know; I just went with the flow in this crazy place.

"Um… How about something to drink…?" I stated almost in question, since I didn't actually know any of the drinks here.

"Okay, what will it be?" He was shining a glass with a dishrag.

"Um, what do you have?"

The man looked a little irritated, but answered my question. "We have ale, rum and goat's milk. …Like it says on the sign behind me."

I felt a little embarrassed and tried to quickly decide on something to get out of his hair. "I'll have, uh …some ale."

The man then turned around and grabbed one of the bottles of gold liquid. He poured part of it into a glass he was cleaning and gave me both. "Here you are."

"How much?" I asked as I took the open bottle and glass.

He told me three scones, and I was pretty sure he didn't mean the tea cake kind. I went into my sack and found the money pouch. I reached inside and pulled out three of the ten square silver coins and gave them to the man.

He took the coins and then asked, "Anything else for you?" After I declined politely, he turned and went back to one of the shelves behind the counter to go back to restocking his wares.

I turned and went over to sit at a round unoccupied table near a window. I took off my backpack and set the bag down on my right side. Then I sat and took a drink from my ale. The alcohol and carbonation in the drink stung a little and the taste was kind of sour and bitter. I had gotten the drink since I figured everyone else in this place was drinking the ale, so I might as well fit in. I had also wanted to try it since I had never gotten to drink beer before. I couldn't understand how adults could drink bottles of this foul stuff all day long back at home. I didn't want to waste it though, especially after I had just paid for it. Maybe I could try goat's milk next time, but it sounded kind of funky to me.

Regardless of the drink choice, everyone was totally into their own world. I could hear many different languages—words spoken in many different tones and cadences. I was lightly startled by one of the customers, a giant burly man, laughing hysterically. Many of the people in the room actually looked back at him, annoyed at the noise.

I took another mouthful of ale, trying to ignore the gross taste, and started to think about all that I had recently experienced and where I was now. What else was in store for me? When I looked outside the window, it was still light out. I wondered how the people in this settlement might see me and if there were other foreign travelers like myself.

I was so engaged in thought that for a brief moment I lost some awareness of what was going on around me. I didn't even notice when some of the other customers in the room had left and different individuals had come in.

I was about half-way done with my drink when someone who looked like another normal human being approached me. He had black hair, a handsome face, tanned olive skin, and he was slim with average muscle tone. He wore a protective suit of dark banded leather. On his right was a sheathed short sword. As he approached the table, he had a glass in his hand. He raised it in a welcoming gesture. He asked me, "You are not from around here?"

I had initially been reaching for my bag on the floor. I wasn't sure about this guy. Since he didn't seem to be dangerous though, I grabbed my own glass, returning the same gesture while replying, "No, not really. Just heading on through."

The man then said, "My name is Jbug. May I sit?" He motioned to the chair sitting across from me.

I nodded, so Jbug pulled the seat out from under the table and sat himself down. He then asked, "What brings you to this area, traveler?"

I quickly gave him a vague response. "I needed a change. I wanted to see what else was out there." I took a nervous sip of my drink, eyes cast down.

Jbug nodded whole-heartedly. "Ah, yes, there is a lot to see! I agree!"

"Are you from around here, Jbug?" His name was a little difficult for me to pronounce and my tongue stumbled over the sound. If my appearance didn't give me away as a foreigner, my accent sure did.

"Yes, a ways down the road, about a mile. I come here to get away from my family or work sometimes." He smiled sheepishly, licking the ale foam from his lips. "Daily life can be absolutely maddening. We all need to clear our minds from the problems we have." He shrugged as he chugged from his glass. "Where are you from, friend?"

"The islands," I blurted out quickly, surprising him and even myself. It seemed like something exotic and far away enough that he might believe that I was merely a traveler from his own world, and not some otherworldly realm.

"Oh! How!?" Jbug's eyes went wide.

Sweat started to prick at my skin, when I realized I had no actual answer to his question. I didn't know anything about any islands here.

I was relieved when Jbug then stopped himself and said, "Oh my. That is so very far from here. You must be very exhausted!"

"Not really…" I replied, eyes darting to the exit. I grabbed my bag and was about to rise from my chair to get away from his prying questions, lest I get found out.

Jbug leaned forward and put a hand on my shoulder and asked me with big, excited eyes, "Can I join you?"

"Uh, sure." I replied, not sure if I should refuse him. The thought occurred that he might be helpful to me if I could learn some things from him about this world.

Smiling warmly, Jbug asked me, "Where are you headed?"

"I'm going north."

After polishing off the rest of my drink, I grabbed my bag, swung it onto my shoulders and headed for the front door. Jbug took a last swig of his ale as well, and followed.

CHAPTER FIVE

As we both headed towards the front door, the man at the counter said, looking at me with a wry smile, "Hope to see you again."

I nodded my head in acknowledgement, though I didn't know what that look was about.

Jbug was holding the door open for me, so I went through. He seemed like a nice guy, but was he friend or foe? I eventually shared my name with him as we walked together.

When we reached the main road, which was about a minute's walk from the door of the tavern, we stopped to ponder a junction. The roads were about fifteen feet wide with a base of dark brown sand and small, brick red rocks. We both turned right with Jbug leading the way. Remembering what he'd said, I asked him, "…Why do you travel this far just to have fun?"

Jbug looked back at me as he answered. "My town really doesn't have a nice place close by where I can relax like this. I also don't want to meet… the wrong type of people."

"What is the 'wrong type' of people?" I wondered if they were dangerous.

"Dwarves and halflings. They're brutes; they just like to get drunk and start fights."

I didn't know what a dwarf was, but I thought it might seem strange to Jbug if I said that. To cover up my ignorance, I stated, "The dwarves in the tavern didn't seem too terrible," hoping that Jbug would agree that at least one was indeed in the tavern.

He replied, "Oh, the couple on the left side of the bar, yes."

I remembered which table he was talking about. At that table were a man and woman, both short and stocky. They basically looked like stout-limbed people who were "vertically-challenged."

Jbug said "Yes, not all dwarves are not bad people. They can be very tough and rowdy when they become angry, though."

My thoughts now wandered to how a halfling would look, and I tried to think of a way to get Jbug give me a hint. We had walked a half mile by now. The road continued straight, and then curved slightly to the right. There were more trees lining the roadsides, smaller and shorter than the ones in the forest. There were numerous small wooded paths that started on the main road and led into the trees to who knew where. While we walked past these paths, I kept up the conversation.

"What's so bad about halflings?" I wondered if they were half human and half something else. "I haven't seen them act like dwarves." I commented.

"No, not as much. There is nothing bad about halflings, per se, though I have met some bad ones." replied Jbug. "The only races you should really be concerned about are gorcs, golgers and gulgaki. These are really evil creatures that roam the land at night, attacking anyone, especially the weak and helpless. Have you ever been attacked by one of these creatures?"

"No. Have you?" I replied.

"I haven't, fortunately, but a friend of mine was. He luckily survived. He was attacked by a gulgaki and managed to escape." A dark look spread across his face. "It took him a long time to recover from his injuries."

"So, how many halflings were in the tavern? I don't think I saw that many."

"I'm not sure, probably several." Jbug, seeing my thoughtful expression, added in lightheartedly, "You know how it's sometimes hard to tell!" He laughed.

I nodded my head in acknowledgement while putting on a smile too, trying to appreciate the humor.

"Elvisa halflings usually are taller with square heads."

I remembered some people with foreheads that were subtly squared. I thought to myself how fortunate I was to have run into someone helpful like Jbug, who was teaching me about this world. He even pointed out different kinds of trees and flowers to me that he said were endemic to this mountainous region.

After a while, I noticed the trees on the paths started to become more stunted in growth. The bases were wider and thicker and more gnarled than the ones I saw in the forest. Intrigued, I decided to take the path I was in front of and see where it led. Jbug asked me where I was going, so I pointed up the trail. His facial expression indicated a clear reluctance.

I asked him, "Do you know where this path goes?"

"It leads to the hills and eventually the town graveyard. There is nothing there—nothing good for you to see there in any case. Why don't you come to my hometown, instead? It makes for a much livelier visit, I assure you."

I weighed the options. I wondered if he was telling the truth, and where his town was, and how long it would take if I went with him. I didn't want to get too sidetracked from my mission. I sensed from Jbug an urgency to go with him back to his town. His obvious discomfort and insistence to leave the trail made me uncomfortable.

I asked Jbug, "Don't you wanna explore it just for fun?"

Jbug replied, "Not really—I'm sure we'll both find it quite boring. I would advise against it."

As he clearly did not want to go, I looked up into the sky and noticed the sun drawing a little lower towards the horizon. It was going to get dark soon. It seemed I could actually see the sun move. I had never seen the sun set so quickly before; I could even see the moon rising and slowly getting brighter.

I decided maybe I ought to go with Jbug so that I might at least have a place to stay for the night before continuing my journey. I figured that he might offer once we got there since he was being so friendly. I asked him, "How far is it to your home?"

He gestured towards the southwest. "It is about two miles from here. Not far at all. So, you would like to come, after all, Lorenz?"

It was more or less the opposite direction I needed to go, but not too far off track, and I needed to rest anyways. I told him yes, and with that, we were off to his house.

We both turned from the entrance of the trail and headed south on the main road. As Jbug and I walked, there were a few minutes of silence. He seemed to have bit more energy in his step. Although I was keeping pace with Jbug, I had an uncomfortable and very bad feeling within my stomach. I didn't really know why my gut was nagging me, but I tried to tell myself I'd trust him. Jbug had been really helpful to me thus far. What could possibly happen?

We finally reached the area of town where Jbug lived: Nidum. He lived on the northern outskirts. There were shops and inns where one could eat and sleep. A local guard stood by, watching the area. He was a human, though pretty big for a human; he was tall, about six feet and five inches, and a bit overweight for his height. He also had a deputy guard working with him. The deputy was also over six feet tall, with dark long hair, and very muscular, but not very bright-looking.

As Jbug and I entered the area, we saw other townspeople on the main road, coming home from work or shopping. As we passed another tavern, we heard a loud laugh. I turned in surprise. Jbug pointed the deputy out to me was as he walked by. The deputy was presumably guffawing about a joke a fellow guardsman had told him—that is, until he saw Jbug.

He stopped cold and gave Jbug a long look. Jbug nodded his head, but the deputy just kept looking at him after glancing at me. That was twice now I'd gotten weird looks since meeting Jbug. I wondered what that was about and I didn't like it one bit.

Jbug and I continued to walk towards his home. I noticed several buildings that were similar in shape and rectangular. The buildings seemed to be made of paneled wood and red brick. It was much darker now with very little daylight left to light the way, so that people are beginning to light up lanterns.

He said to me, "My house is right up this path. We made it just in time."

The path he spoke of was even darker than the main road. There were many trees shading the walkway with their thick, heavy foliage. The path we walked on was only a few feet wide with a bed of dirt, wood chips and leaves. A big old house finally came into view in the shadows at the end of the trail we were following. It was a two-story building with windows to the right and left of the front door that were oval in shape. As we came closer to the house, Jbug's pace quickened.

The home was dark except for the small amount of light coming through the narrow windows. Was this what most homes looked like? Was anyone even at home? I didn't see any family members. In fact, I couldn't see anyone or almost anything at all. My intuition told me to be on my guard.

While Jbug was busy unlocking and opening up the front door, I reached to my backpack to open it. I pulled the small rope to the opening to loosen it and returned my hand to my right side. I did it so quickly that Jbug didn't even notice. I wanted to be ready in case he tried any funny stuff.

He opened the door after fiddling with the key a bit. At the door, I noticed a faint flickering light coming from a candle on a table on the right side of the room. Had he just left that candle burning all day, I wondered. Jbug looked around the room, then looked back at me and said, "Come on in, Lorenz." He held the door open courteously for me to enter.

To the right was a table with wooden chairs. Each chair had high round backs and a circular cushioned seat. There were also small bookcases made of stone. Each shelf was full of dusty books that hadn't been read in years. On the other side of the room was a long rectangular wooden table with two stone saucers on it. On each end were stools and a bench sat close by against the wall. Directly ahead, I noticed stairs that led upward. The stairs were made of old wood that was beginning to splinter. It was hard to imagine that a family lived in this old, dusty place. Before I could glance around more, I was interrupted by Jbug offering me something to drink.

"No thank you, Jbug." I was still satisfied from the drink at the pub earlier.

Jbug stood at the entrance to the staircase. When I had declined his drink, he invited me to go upstairs. "Do you want to go upstairs and see the rest of the house?"

He saw that I was eyeing the old books.

"Those dusty old things are pretty boring, as you can see. Nothing worth looking at! Come on! Let's go upstairs!" Jbug started up the stairs and I didn't have much choice but to follow.

The upstairs hallway led to three rooms. Jbug walked past two rooms and pointed to the one directly ahead of us saying, "This is my room."

I remained on guard and alert as I looked around, following him. At the entrance of Jbug's room, I noticed several small round tables at each corner of the chamber. On each table a single candle was lit to enable us to see throughout the bedroom. Wax was built up messily on the tabletop around each candlestick. Boy, did I miss the convenience of modern day's electricity and light bulbs.

On the north and south side of the room were small bookshelves with numerous books. Already sitting on the edge of the bed in the center of the room, Jbug motioned to me to sit next to him, while he held a book he'd picked up.

I complied, sitting down beside him while placing my backpack on the ground near my feet. I looked at what he had to show me. The book was fairly thick and light brown in color, probably leather bound many years ago. On the cover of the book were two men's faces staring at each other. They had long straight brown hair, square-shaped heads, blue eyes and gloomy expressions. The faces had some resemblances to Jbug's.

"What is this?" I asked him.

Jbug explained that this book was about two of his most famous family members. They were of two of his great uncles. He talked about them having special abilities and how they were never really accepted by their fellow townsfolk because of how different they were from normal people.

Jbug asked me to open the book. I did as he asked. As I opened the cover and turned the pages, he said to me, "Even though this is about my family members, this book helped me figure out where I fit in within my family. It also helped me to figure out what my talents were, so now I know what my purpose in life is."

"That's cool, Jbug. That sounds great." I yawned. The book was kind of boring to look at and I realized that I was beginning to get tired as it had been a very long day. While looking through the book, glancing at the old portraits, I asked Jbug where I could rest for the night.

"You can stay here. There is more than enough room. My family will not be here tonight anyway. You can stay in either of the other rooms. They belong to my children." I thanked him for his hospitality and he nodded in reply with a smile. "Why don't we get something to eat before heading to bed? Can't have you sleeping on an empty stomach! What a poor host I would be! Come, Lorenz, I have some fresh food downstairs."

"Okay, I could go for something hearty."

Jbug led the way merrily. We both headed downstairs and turned for the kitchen.

CHAPTER SIX

This kitchen had a distinct and not very surprising lack of a refrigerator. A large wood-burning stove was the centerpiece of Jbug's kitchen instead. The cooking surface had six round burners. Above the stove hung a wooden cupboard filled with dishes and cookware. On each side of the stove were dark wooden cabinets and counters. A dining table with eight mismatching chairs sat nearby. He must have a surprisingly big family. Noticing this, I asked him, "There must be a lot of people that live here?"

"Not that many people live here, but we frequently have a lot of visitors. My brothers and cousins often stop by for dinner and drinks," Jbug explained. "Some of my cousins are halflings. The rest of my family is human."

My next question had been on my mind for a long while now. "Where is your family right now?" The big, dark, empty house unnerved me. I had been expecting to see a wife and kids.

"They are traveling." He waved his hand dismissively. His answer was too vague.

"Why didn't you go with them?"

"I needed to stay home and watch the house." replied Jbug matter-of-factly. "It is not safe to leave your house unattended for too long."

While we were talking, Jbug had gathered fruit, sliced bread and cheese for us to eat. After placing everything on the table in a big clay bowl, he motioned to me to have a seat.

I sat down in the chair in the corner closest to the door. Jbug then pushed the bowl closer to me and took the chair across from mine. After getting seated, we both started eating. While taking a bite of some creamy pungent cheese I had placed on a slice of bread, I asked him, "Where did they travel to?"

"They went to a town far away to visit an in-law. It's quite boring, really. I never really like to go there." He was still being vague.

After eating an apple and some more slices, my stomach was pleasantly full and I felt sleepy. I wanted to get some rest so I could continue the journey, even though I had other questions to ask. I hinted that I wanted to go up to bed by yawning loudly, covering my mouth.

Jbug commented, "You must be tired."

"Yeah," I said. "I think I'm going to head up to bed. Thanks for everything." I then excused myself and headed out the kitchen door, immediately turning to head up the stairs.

As I left the kitchen, Jbug told me with a smile, "Good night, Lorenz."

I went up the stairs and into the little bedroom near Jbug's room.

Jbug watched me leave. Little did I know, while we were walking to Jbug's house, he had sent signals to his partners hiding in the shrubs and darkness nearby that he had found another victim.

In town, Jbug had a bad reputation of being a no-good thug. He had a history befriending and inviting weary travelers to his home to take advantage of them. The other rooms in the house were not actually for Jbug's family members, as he would tell his guests. The rooms were for his partners in crime.

The scheme they used on the unsuspecting guests worked quite well. During the night, while the tired guest slept, he and his comrades would assault and rob their victims. The plan was working very well for him thus far. When Jbug heard me get to the top of the stairs, he motioned to his partners who were standing outside the house, peeking in through the windows, to come inside. I didn't even hear the front door open downstairs.

As I entered my room, I noticed it was dimly lit by one lonely candle by the back wall on the floor. I had a decent sized bed, maybe queen-sized, covered in a frayed quilted blanket. Familiar bookshelves rested against the walls. It was a sort of small room, and smelled a little musty, but it was fine.

While I was upstairs, preparing for bed, Jbug and his partners were planning their attack. His companions, Mannu and Nathanu—both fairly tall and burly humans—had quietly entered the house, meeting Jbug in the kitchen. They both carried knives and wore dark leather clothing which consisted of rugged pants and thick sleeveless shirts.

Jbug told them when they first arrived, to be quiet because I was resting upstairs. He reviewed the plan with them, which was to wait till I fell asleep. Jbug would then slip into the room, and drop magical control dust over me, and then say a spell, rendering me helpless.

The room I was in happened to be Mannu's room. It was pretty bleak and there were no personal effects in the room to really indicate that this was a child's room. The idea kind of bothered me, but I was too tired to question it or think about leaving. Looking at the bed caused me to feel even more exhausted.

I got into the bed which was a little hard, but bearable. The blanket was musty from the body odor of whoever used it and the old fabric was scratchy. I initially positioned my bag on the bed next to me such that my sword was easy to reach, but on second thought, I decided to take my sword out and lay it next to me, concealed under the blanket.

While lying in bed, I began to think about all of my recent experiences. I thought about how different this world was compared to my own. I thought about the voice that spoke to me and what the voice told me to do, and the magical gem that brought me here. When I would go back…? After that thought, I drifted off into slumber.

After hearing nothing but silence for a long while, Jbug, Nathanu, and Mannu got up from the table where they were all were sitting and rummaged through the cupboards. They reached in and pulled out soft rabbit-skin shoes. They all took off their heavy travelling boots and slipped the soft rabbit-skin on, as they could walk in them stealthily without making a sound.

Jbug slowly crept up the stairs, followed by Mannu and Nathanu. When he reached the door of the bedroom and heard only deep breathing, he motioned for to them to come up. They did so, as quietly as they could.

Jbug looked inside the room and saw that I was sound asleep. He slowly entered the room, approaching the bed. At that point, he reached into his trouser pocket and pulled out a small satchel. Mannu came into the room and walked to the other side of the bed. Jbug, holding the pouch in his left hand, reached in and grabbed a handful of what looked like light blue sparkling dust with his right. He pulled out his right hand with a handful of the particles and held them over my head. He just needed to sprinkle the powder and say the incantation: "Sleep, sleep, sleep so deep. You will do whatever I speak." This spell would enchant the victim into obeying whatever the spell caster said.

Nathanu had now entered the room and was at the foot of the bed. The entire bed was surrounded. Mannu and Nathanu looked on with excitement.

Being a light sleeper, and having been so suspicious of Jbug's behavior, I was slowly waking up from having the three big men walking around me. I could hear their heavy, nervous breathing. I knew that one had to be Jbug, but I wondered who else was in the room.

I was alarmed, but stayed very still and controlled my breathing to be slow to make it sound as if I were still asleep. The robbers were not aware that I was now awake and listening to them with my eyes closed.

I sensed someone looming over me. I decided I needed to act because I was in trouble. I felt my heart start beating faster. The hairs on my entire body were standing on end. My gut twisted itself in knots, trying to make me do something.

Jbug's right hand, which had the dust in it, was over my head. He was about to open his fingers to release the powder and even started saying the incantation, "Sleep, sleep," when his focus shifted suddenly from the chant to my sword that was now pointed at him as I sat straight up in the bed and tossed away the covers.

Mannu and Nathanu were both so stunned that they were unable to move for a moment. At that point, I jerked the tip of my sword towards Jbug, so that he got the message to back away from me.

His hand was still frozen in the same position when he started to move away from the bed. I got up from the bed, placing my feet on the floor, keeping Jbug at a sword's length away from me. I silently motioned to Jbug to give me the small pouch. Jbug slowly extended his left hand to me with the pouch, his right hand still in the same position, holding the powder.

While focused on Jbug, I was still aware of the other two in the room. They remained motionless, watching what was happening. Evidently, Jbug and his partners had done this plan so many times without a hitch, that they were surprised and didn't know what to do now in this situation.

I grabbed the pouch from Jbug. I then motioned to him to turn his hand, with the dust in it, towards the floor. I didn't want him scheming to throw it at me. He began to turning his hand towards the floor, letting the shining dust fall. All of a sudden, he decided to pull back his hand and attempt to toss the dust into my face.

He tried to pull a fast one, but I was faster. As Jbug pulled back his hand, I drew back my sword enough to get some momentum and struck Jbug's wrist as it came towards me. Before Jbug realized it, his right hand was falling to the floor with the dust flying out in a blue sparkling puff. I took several steps back to avoid the dust as Jbug clutched his wrist and fell to his knees writhing and crying in pain.

At that moment, Nathanu closest, moved towards Jbug. I immediately raised my sword, still red with blood on it, towards Nathanu. Out of the corner of my right eye, I noticed Mannu's body tense as if to take action. I maintained the sword at Nathanu, but turned my head towards Mannu, letting him know he better not try anything. Mannu stopped immediately, yet his facial expression showed he was furious.

Nathanu took this opportunity to run out of the room.

I was extremely surprised at the ease in which the sword cut through flesh and bone and how fast it could swing, yet I had no time to linger on this thought. I was in grave danger. I was glad that I had these abilities as I realized I probably would have been killed by these three treacherous men.

After Nathanu left the room, I told Mannu to move to the other side. As Mannu started to move, he stepped back towards the bookshelf while keeping his eyes on me. Jbug moaned again in pain briefly, distracting me. This allowed Mannu to grab his short sword he had hidden behind his little bookshelf. Jbug's eyes closed and his body went limp.

While watching Mannu, I lightly poked Jbug's body with my foot to see if he was still alive. His body didn't move. He was probably unconscious from the shock of the injury. I quickly stepped over him to get into a better position to defend myself, as I was cornered where I was currently standing. I also listened for Nathanu, who had run out of the room moments ago.

As Mannu began to advance towards me, I pushed over a small table close by to obtain more space. Nathanu had not returned yet, but I could hear the sound of metal dragging from outside of the room entrance at the end of the hall. I knew that I had to act quickly otherwise or else I would be overwhelmed by the two big men if they were to attack me together at once.

I lunged as fast as I could, and surprised Mannu. I held my sword over my head with both hands as if I was going to come down on Mannu's head. He raised his sword to block this attack, and the blades clashed. The poor parry, however, carried the force of my blade down, nicking the side of his right inner thigh with a deep gash. Mannu fell to the ground dropping his sword in pain and clutching his bleeding leg.

I immediately turned around in preparation of facing Nathanu. Just then Nathanu came to the entrance of the room with his own sword drawn.

He screamed at me, "You will die for this!"

I was cornered in the small room, by the bed and a hunched Mannu. As Nathanu charged towards me, I dove for the bed, rolling over it and landing on the other side of it on the opposite end of the room. I was now facing Nathanu with my back to the far wall and my sword drawn.

Nathanu again charged at me, roaring. My sword was in position for blocking Nathanu's blow. Blocking each of Nathanu's attacks, I waited for the right opening to make my own. Nathanu's attacks were very strong and forceful, yet they were easy to parry with my lightweight sword.

It seemed that despite its lack of weight, my sword was able to bear the force Nathanu offered and I didn't lose much ground in the fight. The sword must have some special power to enable me to fight so effectively. Finally, the opening came when Nathanu's attacks stopped as he tripped over the small table in front of him that I had pushed over. His sword was pointed to the floor for a brief moment.

Seizing the opportunity, I drew back my sword as far as I could and swung my sword towards Nathanu's midsection. Before Nathanu could block my sword appropriately, with one fell swoop, I hit the gripping fingers of his sword hand, as he tried to raise his blade to block me, my blade clanging off his sword's hilt after slicing through bone.

Immediately, Nathanu yelled out in pain. He grabbed his wound with his other hand, screaming and fell to his knees. I then approached Nathanu with the tip of my sword lightly touching his neck.

I asked Nathanu, "Why did you do this? Who are you?"

He did not respond. He just looked at me with hatred in his eyes. I put a little more pressure on his neck.

"Do I have to ask again?"

Nathanu responded by moving his head slightly side to side, to communicate no, gritting his teeth from his rage and pain. He started out with, "Jbug is the leader. It was his idea that we could make money by robbing the newcomers to this remote area. Jbug would scout out foreign travelers to trick."

I released some of the pressure room my sword's tip and listened as he continued. I was seething still with anger and adrenaline of my own.

Nathanu continued. "When Jbug finds someone, he befriends them. Eventually, he brings them here."

"Why?" I asked with unhidden anger in my voice.

"Money. Once they are in our house, he puts them to sleep with his powder and takes all of their possessions."

"His powder?"

"Yes," his eyes flicked over to the sparkling blue dust scattered across the floor. "You drop this dust over the person while they are asleep. This dust puts them into a deep trance. They do whatever you tell them."

"Where did Jbug get this dust?"

Nathanu hesitated.

I put the edge of my sword back at his throat. I didn't know if I could trust him, but I figured I should listen to what he had to say.

Nathanu closed his eyes and remained silent, lips pursed tightly in distress. When I pressed a little harder to nudge him to continue, he shouted, "All right! All right! We got it from an old cigamian's home."

"Where is this cigamian?" I demanded, pulling the sword away again.

"He's probably dead by now," said Nathanu. "But his house is in the next town over. It's on the hillside between two large rocks. It's a large dark grey house. It's about two miles south from the town and a half mile east from the main road. It's the only big house on the hill, I promise you. You cannot miss it."

Nathanu's hand continued to bleed as he grimaced and choked out the words in pain. After telling me where the house was, he groaned and slumped to the ground, unconscious.

CHAPTER SEVEN

After watching Nathanu fall unconscious, I looked around. For the first time, I had a moment to take in what happened within the last few minutes. I was really surprised at my fighting abilities. Many questions arose. How did I do this? What magic was involved? Did the voice have anything to do with what just happened? I didn't have the answers.

I decided to focus on what lay before me—the three bandits. I didn't know if they were alive or not, so I thought I had better check.

I looked at Nathanu. He was unconscious, but still alive after checking his pulse. I stepped around Nathanu and headed towards Mannu.

As I approached Mannu carefully, I looked for any signs of movement checking his pulse and chest. He was alive. The wound from where his upper leg was sliced continued to bleed a lot, yet slower as it continued to spill onto the wood floor. I didn't initially think it was a serious wound, but it seemed he'd gotten weak from the loss of blood; I might have hit a vessel.

I left Mannu and approached Jbug. There were no signs of life in the trickster. He was thin and panicked and had bled out quickly. I felt guilt and alarm well up inside me; I had only tried to protect myself. I hadn't intended to kill anyone.

It was still dark outside when I decided I had better check to see if they had any useful things on them. There might be something that would lead me to the cigamian whom they'd robbed and killed.

I bent down to check Jbug's pockets. I started with Jbug's right pocket in his trousers. I found another small pouch still filled with some of the dust. I checked the left pocket and found a piece of paper which contained instructions on how to use the dust. I placed the instructions in my bag which was still lying on the floor. I also took about a dozen gold pieces that were sitting in his pocket, no doubt gained by his illicit activities. I then went over to search Mannu.

First, I looked at the sword Mannu used. The blade of the sword was sharp and was about as long as mine. There were no significant markings on the blade or the handle. I thought to take it just in case I could use it for anything, or at least so that he wouldn't do anymore evil with it. I put the sword on the bed for the moment. I went through his pockets, finding more gold pieces and kept them for myself too. He didn't stir.

Next, I examined Nathanu's sword. His sword was slightly longer and wider than Mannu's. The blade was very sharp as well. It also had designs engraved on the blade. Towards the tip of the blade was a symbol that looked like a horse with a rider on it waving a sword. The design was small, but large enough to see clearly. On the bottom of the blade towards the handle was a symbol of two swords crossing. I decided to keep this sword too. I was impressed with all the engravings, but I found nothing else of interest.

I grabbed my bag and put all of the weapons and money away. I decided to check this room and the other rooms in the house for more spoils since they obviously had been robbing people for a while and might have more useful things hidden in the house.

I started with the bed. I lifted up the mattress. There, I found nothing but hair and dust balls. Between all their robbing and plundering, it seemed the bandits never got around to any spring cleanings. I stepped away from the bed, now focusing on the bookshelf near Mannus' unconscious body.

I noticed the books on the shelves. "The Hill of the Tinia" had a conspicuous spine. I opened the book and read a few pages and found it to be of no use to me, as it was just some kind of children's storybook. If there was a kid's book here, I wondered if the robbers had taken this house from a real family and if they were okay. I then remembered Mannu reaching behind the shelf to get the sword. I carefully moved the shelf to check behind it, being wary of any possible booby traps.

Behind the shelf I found nothing except the floor, which needed a good sweeping, so I decided to check Jbug's room since it was close by. I started with the bed as I did in the other room. I lifted up the covers and mattress and found nothing. I then went over to the bookcase and looked closely at the books inside. There was nothing good. This was getting a little predictable. All my searching was getting me nowhere.

I then started to move the bookcase to the right a few inches when I heard the sound of something metal hitting the floor. I looked on the floor in front of the case, but couldn't find what had fallen. I pulled the bookcase further away from the wall that it was up against and found something shiny and gold on the floor. They were a pair of ornate golden keys on a key ring. Score!

I didn't know what they were for, so I would just have to try them out. I took the keys, got up, and went to the door at the entrance of the room. I looked at the keys to see if they would fit into the keyhole in the door since they both seemed similar in shape. The front of the key went in with no resistance, but only reached about halfway into the keyhole before it stopped.

I turned the key left and right, but it did not go any further. I applied more force, but it still wouldn't budge. I pulled the key out and turned the key upside down to see if it would go in. That just made it worse. I then realized that these keys might not even be for this house, so I placed the keys in my pocket. They might be for the cigamian's house which they had robbed. I decided to check the last bedroom just in case there might be something.

I backed out of Jbug's room, scanning everything in order to make sure I didn't miss anything. Once out of the room, I went down the hall. I heard a moan and a rustle from the coming from the next room where Jbug, Mannu and Nathanu were. Immediately I prepared myself by holding up my sword.

Nathanu had revived and was attempting to attack me in blind rage, like a rabid animal. He was somehow able to stand up, gain his balance and attempted to lunge forward towards me with his one good fist; he had no weapon since I had taken his sword. I was able to easily move out of the way since he was hurt and clumsy. He crashed into the door frame and seemed to fall unconscious again. I decided I better leave the house and skipped searching the last room. I didn't want to be around then when they woke up again.

I went downstairs to quickly gather some of their food and leave. I kept my sword in the ready position, not knowing if there were more of them lurking about the house. I reached the last step with the entire living room in full sight and thankfully saw no one. I then turned left and headed for the kitchen.

I remembered where the food was stored from when Jbug pulled out food from the cabinets for the two of us to eat. It was a shame that he seemed like such a nice man at first, but had actually turned out to be a dangerous robber.

I looked into the cabinets and I grabbed a loaf of bread, some fruits and cheese, and was pleased to even find some dried jerky meats. I arranged them quickly into a burlap sack on the counter, which I then put into my bag, before walking out the kitchen door. Needless to say, my backpack started to become heavy from all the things I had taken from Jbug's house. Luckily, the bag had enough separators, pockets and compartments to keep all of the items I had fairly organized.

Before leaving, I listened for any sounds coming from upstairs or out in the living area and looked around the room one last time, seeing if I missed anything important or of value. Then I stepped outside. I hoped that the cigamian's house was not too long a walk away.

The air outside was crisp and chilly, yet not too cold. It was now very early in the morning. The day light increased as the large suns rose in the east.

I knew that I had to continue my quest for the Creator, but I felt I couldn't pass up the chance to get such useful tools to help me in my journey. He did tell me that I would acquire helpful tools, and this magical dust sounded very helpful.

I approached the main road and I turned south on the road towards the next town. Other people who were walking along the main road either looked at me briefly or ignored me. I made sure not to look suspicious. I turned and headed towards the next town, to the cigamian's home.

As I walked, I noticed the various different races of people walking along the path. There were short, tall, large-bodied, small-bodied and different colored types walking all over the place.

I also noticed that there weren't many buildings along the path, but there were many trees. There were also many tree stumps along the road, obviously from people cutting them down for some easy lumber.

Alongside the trees, connecting to the main path were also smaller paths that would lead away into the groves. Maybe these smaller paths led to homes. Nathanu did say that the cigamian's home was accessible by a path off of the main road.

The main road was lined with thick trees. The lobed leaves from their branches were of a deep emerald green and the shapes resembled diamonds. The branches were full of these verdant leaves and hung low. The trees were equidistant except for the places where the paths exited, that led up to the homes.

As I walked along the path, I remembered the many things that happened in the last several days: the voice in the tree hollow, meeting Jbug, then almost being killed by the guy I thought was my friend, and how it was that I was able to fight like I did. Well, I was glad to know that I could defend myself.

I then had a flashback of times when I had trouble protecting myself from cruel bullies. How much sweeter it would have been if I had these abilities and strength then. I guarantee that no one would have messed with me.

I had been involved in these thoughts so much that I had not realized that I had walked over a mile and passed several buildings. Was this the right village?

I immediately looked up into the hills and spotted the top of what looked like a castle or big grey house between two stony outcroppings. As I got closer, I saw what looked like a break in the trees leading up to the castle.

Right as I took my first step to start up the path, all of a sudden, there was a flurry of pitch black darkness and I got that queasy feeling that I was traveling somewhere.

I had been transported back to my real world. How was that even possible? I didn't even touch the gem. The Creator had told me that I would be able to travel between the worlds in different ways, but this surprised me. After a few moments, I landed on my feet and the sinking, tingling feeling faded away. I tried to recognize where I was.

I realized first that the gem was still in my pocket. Also, I was no longer in the schoolyard where I had left off, but in a completely different school—a much nicer one!

New memories flooded suddenly into me in vivid flashes of sound and images in my mind. I was no longer living with my aunt. Darius and I had just moved back and was now living with my mother again. Prior to living with my mom, my brother and I had lived with my aunt for several months while my mother worked odd hours, saving up money and sending part to her sister Georgia.

After a few minutes, I remembered where I was and what was going on. I was at a different school near my mother's home in the same grade. It was still the same school year. I looked around and realized I was on a grass field with my new schoolmates. It was now recess and we were out playing kickball. There were the sounds of other students playing and chatting everywhere.

A classmate on my team, a short African American boy with a shaved head, standing behind me said, "Lorenzo, go ahead. What're you waiting for?"

I turned around, and looked at the ball, which had been rolled to me. I nodded and kicked the ball with all my might, sending it flying faster than I had ever seen it go! My kick propelled the red rubber ball easily past the second base person.

I immediately ran towards first base where the first baseman was waiting for the ball as I ran past him. The second baseman had left his base plate to fetch the ball which was still rolling swiftly away from him. He wouldn't be able to get to the ball in time to stop me.

I ran all the way around to second base. The second baseman had finally reached the ball. As the he was preparing to throw the ball to tag me out, I was already halfway towards third base. After he threw the ball towards third, as if in slow-motion, I saw that the ball would surely hit me and tag me out if I kept going. With the ball only split moments away from me, I stopped abruptly and the bouncy red ball flew right by me, past the third baseman into the north end of the playground. Surprised, the third baseman bolted after ball, leaving his base open.

I touched third base and then started for home. As I approached the home base, the third baseman had reached the ball and had thrown it towards home. I had misjudged how quickly he could run. It looked as if I wouldn't make it to home base in time thanks to his excellent pitch which had sent the ball flying straight and true.

I was only seconds away from home base when I noticed the ball soaring quickly towards home base. Standing at home was a friend whom I had recently met. His name was Mike. He stood about five feet tall, about my height. He stood at the base, poised to catch the ball. It was clear that I would be tagged out because the ball was going to reach the base moments before I would.

I was two feet from the base when the ball arrived home. Mike, standing right next to the base, caught the ball—no, he didn't! He fumbled, and the ball slipped through his fingers, and bounced on his knee, rolling about seven feet away from him. His team members groaned loudly in annoyance as he chased after the red ball.

He left the home base wide open for me to reach. By the time Mike had fetched the ball, I had already tagged the base. I was safe and had scored the winning point just before recess could end.

I cheered and pumped my fists in the air with my team members, showing my great excitement and happiness. I couldn't believe that I made it this far. We had never seen a home run like this before. My teammates congratulated me and slapped me jovially on the back, exclaiming at what a great play it was.

The other team wasn't as excited. Actually, they were pretty unhappy with Mike, and were shouting angrily at him, because he had allowed me to score. Mike's teammates teased and booed him, telling him how they wouldn't choose him on their teams again. Tears welled up in his eyes at the mean-spirited words, but that only made the children taunt him more. I didn't notice the negativity on the other team as I was too busy celebrating with mine.

I didn't know it at the time, but Mike was mad at me for scoring. Mike and I were friends, I thought, but he was miserable and embarrassed and felt that this was somehow my fault.

I was no longer celebrating and now was heading back to my classroom. I smiled to Mike, not realizing that Mike was actually angry with me. He decided to make his move after seeing me turn around and start for the line to head back to class.

He shoved me while I wasn't looking, using both of his hands as hard as he could. I was surprised by this sudden attack and lost my balance, flailing my arms and almost falling down. I gave him an astonished look. I glanced to see if any adults were looking in our direction and within a matter of seconds, I angrily shoved Mike back.

"What's your problem, Mike?!" I cried.

He wasn't prepared for this either and fell to the ground, scraping his hands as he landed.

By the time he scrambled back up onto his feet, I had left Mike and was heading to my classroom, ignoring him. He had yelled out in shock and pain when he landed, drawing the attention of a few students nearby who walked on after looking at him. Eventually, a yard supervisor came over to his aid.

She asked Mike, "What's wrong?"

Desperate to try to get me into trouble, he pouted and pointed in my direction. "Lorenzo, that boy there, pushed me!"

The teacher tried to look in my direction too, but it was impossible to pick me out amongst the other students heading back. "Who was it?"

Mike just whined and kept pointing.

The yard supervisor, exasperated from Mike's childish behavior, patted him on the back and said to him, "I can't pick him out right now. Just get back to class and I can talk with your teacher about this later."

Mike was now just grumbling and pouting, but went and joined his class line which was heading into his building. Once I had entered my classroom, I took a second to quickly glance back to see what had happened. Looking through the closing door, I saw Mike returning to his classmates. The woman who had talked to Mike was heading back to her own class. I exhaled a sigh of relief.

Once inside, I overheard a couple of kids complain that they hadn't gotten the chance to use the restroom before recess was over. My teacher sighed and then encouraged the students to go to the bathroom before she started the lesson.

The girls went in the direction of the girl's bathroom and the boys went towards the boy's bathroom, just about a minute's walk away. The other boys and I were laughing and talking on the entire way. Some of them recapped the events of the epic kickball play I had made, which made me glow with pride.

After getting to the restroom, the other boys headed to urinals to do their business, so I walked up to one as well, carefully spacing myself away from the others being used.

When I had finished and washed my hands, I turned to leave the bathroom with my classmates when I felt something buzzing in my right pocket.

What could it be now?

CHAPTER EIGHT

I immediately went into one of the stalls in the boy's bathroom. After entering the stall, I closed the stall door and waited a minute or two. All the students had by now left the bathroom. I reached into my pocket, grabbed the brightly shining gem and looked at it. As I watched it, its purple glow intensified, gleaming throughout the entire bathroom.

I heard the voices of students walking past the bathroom start to fade. At that moment, I was getting that sinking feeling like I was on a rollercoaster ride.

I closed my eyes and let the feeling wash over me. When I opened them, I had landed on the edge of a dirt path. This path was surrounded by green sloping hills covered with bright green grass and tall trees. There were no other buildings around as I surveyed the area. When I turned to the north, I noticed the large grey house I had found earlier.

The house sat nestled in the side of a hill, somewhat hidden. The windows were rectangular in shape. The door was the same and it was on the far right side of the house. I saw no one else around.

I once again started up the path towards the building. The path bed was made of dirt, broken tree limbs and wood chips. Above me, the suns shone bright and high in the morning sky, partially covered by light pink clouds.

About a minute later, I could see the house clearly. While from afar, the house appeared hazily grey, when I got closer, I could see that the front of the house was decorated in green wood panels with red trim. There were countless eerie wood carvings of smiling faces decorating the house's exterior. The wooden visages were each about as big as my hand and each wore a different smiling expression. I had never seen anything like this before. This bizarre design puzzled me and interested me to enter the house to see what could be inside. As I approached the bottom of the stairs to the house, I decided to keep my sword out just in case.

The stairs leading up the house were made of wide grey brick with flecks of green stone embedded within them. I carefully made my way slowly towards the door. The front door was huge, about twelve feet tall made of solid wood. Its handle was made of what looked like dark metal and it was shaped like a star. It was actually a pretty charming shape for a door knob.

The door itself was painted purple and decorated with gold leaf trim stretching several inches all around the edges. In the center was a big design that looked like a flying lion with its wings spread, growling towards something that looked like the sun.

I noticed what looked like a keyhole under the door handle. I bent down, moving closer to the door to see if I could see anything through it. I could see only darkness.

More curious, I raised my sword such that the tip was pointed towards the front door and I pushed it. All of a sudden, I felt and heard the door creak and then come open.

My body froze, not knowing what would happen. I pulled my sword back from the door and raised it in preparation to wield it, ready for what horrors might come from inside. After Jbug and company, I couldn't trust any strange empty houses anymore. After a few seconds, nothing happened, so I took my sword again and pressed it against the door to push it open all the way.

With the sunlight now streaming in, I could see household furniture. I squinted with my eyes, trying to identify anything else in there. After placing my head through the door to peek in better, I could see that it was a really large space with a very high ceiling. The room was probably large enough to fit all the students of my entire elementary school. I could see many things including chairs, tables, chests and other objects. I kept my guard up, but decided it would be okay to go inside. My instincts told me that it seemed safe to enter.

Finally, I could see how large the room really was. The light coming from the door was the only thing illuminating the entire room because all of the windows were all closed and shuttered. To my left, against the wall, was a large bench with cushions. The bench was of a deep, lustrous purple color, the likes of which I had never seen before. The velvety padding on the seat and the back of the bench was thick and black. In front of the bench were several oak tables covered with what looked like silk fabric on top. On top each small table was an unlit candle in a lime green holder. Next to the candles on each table were many glass vials filled with a green liquid. Was this some kind of research laboratory? If it was, whoever was in charge certainly had strange taste in interior decorating.

An incredible lavish rug woven in colorful fibers complimenting the color scheme of the room was spread out across the floor. The walls were draped in fine purple and pink linen. The rest of the room's walls were lined with long book shelves. At the back of the room were two doors that seemed to head to other parts of the house.

I remained vigilant, ready for any sudden movement. I had learned my lesson from the last encounter when I was almost killed. I didn't want to risk anything. I knew now that I couldn't be too careful in a stranger's house.

All of a sudden, I heard a faint creaking noise. I looked around the room to see where it was coming from. I turned to see that the front door was closing behind me.

I immediately leapt towards the closing door handle to stop it. It was my only source of light! I didn't make it; my leap stopped short and I missed the handle. I fell to the floor flat on my stomach with a painful thud. My sword fell to the floor with a loud clang while the front door clicked shut. The room had become totally dark.

I slowly got up, remembering where I was and what was next to me. I pushed myself up from the floor after feeling around for my sword which I'd dropped. I found I was panting with fear, so I softened my breathing and calmed myself down, trying to think with a clear head. I would grope slowly through the darkness until I found the front door again, open it and prop it open with a rock or something.

Right at that moment, the candles on the tables lit up. The flame on each candle was big and bright yellow, lighting up the entire room. I could now see everything in here just fine. Was it some kind of automatic reaction the magic candles had to darkness? I walked past all of the tables with candles on them, making sure I touched nothing. I made my way through the room to a door on the other side.

I stepped forward and then pressed my ear close to the door, wondering if I would hear anything behind it. It was completely silent, so I grabbed the round bronze door handle and turned it clockwise. The first thing I heard was the door creaking and the lock clicking as I opened it. I pulled the door towards myself slowly, making sure to brace myself for attack. I stepped out from behind the door, standing right in the middle of the opening. My sword was ready and in place to protect me from any harm. My eyes then widened after I saw what was inside.

After I fully opened the door, I stepped inside the new room. It was absolutely amazing! I was so stunned at what I saw that my jaw dropped and I nearly dropped my sword as well. I went inside the room, my eyes flitting around everywhere.

The color scheme in this room was similar to the other one, but everything here was brighter and much more vibrant. A wide majestic spiral staircase about eight feet wide, flanked by a gold banister ornamented with royal purple circles sat in the middle of this room. The staircase wound up to a higher level in this huge house. Charmed by the architectural beauty, I started up the gilded staircase.

As I ascended the stairs, I paid close attention to the walls adorned in purple and gold linen strips of wallpaper. On the lofty high ceiling were paintings of men in all sorts of impressive uniforms and exotic hats. The hats were round, square, rectangular, blue and red and other shapes and colors—probably status symbols. The various men had long, short, or wide noses. They had big, small or wide eyes. I wondered who all these men were, that they would be painted on the ceiling of this strange mansion.

The walls were also covered in similar colors and hanging on nails on the festive walls were portraits. These pictures were of more important-looking men in suits. I imagined that these might be paintings of those who had lived previously in this house. I looked at these pictures and the intricate ceiling as I continued to climb the spiraling stairs.

At the top of the stairwell was a tall, dark hallway that continued straight. It looked like there was another hallway leading off to the right. I had never seen anything as opulent or elaborate as this mansion in all of my life. I wondered to myself how many millions of dollars it would cost to build a house like this.

When I reached the top step, I stopped immediately due to the sudden lighting of the numerous candles along the walls. Things in this world seemed to have a habit of activating automatically, which unnerved me. I wondered what kind of magic made it so that the candelabra of the mansion could spontaneously light like that when someone entered the room.

The candleholders were about eighteen inches tall, sleek and painted purple. They were molded with smiling faces like the spooky house trim outside. The candles themselves were about ten inches tall and made of what looked like gold.

I immediately looked for movement and listened for sounds in the huge abandoned house. As I looked down the hallway directly in front of me, I could see other doors. The second hallway looked basically like a replica of the other. Everything was still and quiet. All that could be seen down both halls was the same—lit candelabra and doors on each side.

Which way should I go? With so many doors to examine, I had nothing to lose starting my search now. I arbitrarily decided to go down the hall to my right. Down this hall, there were four sets of wall candles, one on each side of the hall. In between each set of wall candles was a large door.

After taking one step to my right, the candles starting flickering all of a sudden as if a gust of wind had blown past. I immediately stopped. The wall lights stopped flickering. I took another step down the hall towards the first set of wall candles. The candles again began to flicker erratically. The flames flickered every time I moved. It was creepy, but I had to deal with it. I walked towards the first wall candle to my right.

I looked at the dancing flame and the holder. The candelabrum had the design of a face with a wide open mouth on the bottom where the candle was inserted. The mouth and eyes of this face were lit up as well. I wondered how they could possibly glow so brightly with the candle's flame being at the top. I inspected the candleholders, pressing on them to see if there was a secret lever or button or something.

After inspecting the wall candle and finding nothing, I decided to move on to the door that was closest to the candle I was standing by, the flame flickering eerily behind me, casting irregular shadows. I was about three feet away from the door when the lights stopped flickering. I immediately stopped. I felt something wasn't right.

"What's going on?" I asked aloud. Nothing was down the hallway. I turned around to face the direction I came from. There was still nothing in that direction. I then tried to see if I could hear anything. When I heard nothing but a long silence, I had no choice but to press on, despite the beads of nervous sweat beading up on my forehead and the back of my neck. The spooky house was really getting to me.

I approached the door and was surprised to find that it was actually slightly ajar.

"Oh!" I exclaimed. I stepped back and gripped my sword with both hands.

After a moment of waiting and breathing hard, nothing burst out of the room. I took the end of my sword and used it to push the door open slowly. As it swung open, I saw the vague silhouettes of furniture in the darkness room. I suddenly had the urge to go in and explore.

Candles along the walls of the room lit up. Strewn all over the entire chamber were furniture and other household objects turned over, broken and shattered. The room was utterly demolished. The carpets were torn, the wallpaper was charred, and tablecloths were ripped to shreds. Almost none of the furnishings had survived. The pieces that littered the ground were mostly remains of chairs and tables turned over, broken and even burnt.

It looked as if there had been a major fight in this room. As I surveyed the room, I thought of Jbug's house and the incident that had occurred there. I suddenly realized that someone might be hurt and lost in the rubble here.

"Is anyone here? Are you okay?" I called out into the gloom.

I looked around the room seeing if I could find a body or an injured person. While looking around, I noticed a door on the far right corner of the room intentionally blocked by broken piles of furniture. Someone could be trapped behind it!

With my sword drawn, I carefully walked towards the blocked door. I walked around or stepped over broken and burned pieces of glass and furniture to get to the door. I wondered how the wooden things had gotten so burned without the entire house going up in flames.

Standing right before the jammed door, I heard something move behind me. I immediately spun around and the door to the entrance of the room shut itself closed with an audible click. Why were the doors closing? Was there anything in the room? Was I trapped in here? After looking around, nothing was moving. I didn't know if there was someone hiding nearby, if magic was afoot, or if it was just a coincidence, but I focused on the blocked door. I had to open it. I pulled the pieces of furniture away from the door with my strong arms, removing the obstruction.

The poor door was marred with gouges and soot. I grabbed its square knob and slowly turned it. I was careful as I didn't want to startle whatever might be trapped behind the door. When I opened the door a crack, I found I could not see anything inside because it was completely dark and the only light shining in was from the faint candlelight from this room.

As I opened the door even more, I could see that it appeared to be some kind of storage closet. I saw several crates of varying sizes on the right side of the room, stacked about three feet high. There were more dark wooden crates aligned against the wall. The entire room was filled with boxes except for the very back wall, where in between the crates, lying on the hardwood floor was what looked like a big, tied-up sack, ominously large enough to fit a person inside. It gave me the creeps. I hesitated about entering the room.

I stepped inside and stopped to get a better view of the unnerving bundle, whatever it was. I approached it with great curiosity as well as great anxiety, wary of any unpleasant surprises. It appeared to be a big bag that looked like it could be filled with something like a mound of clothing—or a body. The bag was made of dark blue linen and was bulbous from whatever was inside.

There was a flicker coming from the light through the door. I spun around to face the door briefly to make sure no one was there in the other room. When I turned back around to face the bag on the ground again, it looked like it had moved several inches to the side. It couldn't have moved! I looked around the room again to see if anyone or anything could have done it. No one appeared to be in the room with me.

"Did anything else move?" I whispered breathily to myself. I looked closely at all of the boxes and crates. Nothing else was different. I then returned my gaze to the ominous sack in question. I prepared myself; I was ready to destroy whatever was inside if it meant harm.

Now the bulbous bag did begin to move more. It wriggled left and right a few inches, struggling back and forth. When it began moving, I stepped back and was ready with my sword. Due to its shifting around, I could see the top of the bag was tied tightly shut with coils of thick rope all around it.

Needing to see what was inside, I took my sword, being careful not to hurt whatever was trapped within as it continued to wiggle and roll around, and used the blade to try and cut the rope. I wedged the tip of the sword into the knot, and it loosened readily when I worked at it with some effort.

The rope began to unwind and the bag started to open a little. It stopped moving around. It was as if whatever was in the bundle knew what was happening.

I began to worry since if it was a person that was inside, I imagined that he or she would have said something to me by now. It had been silent this whole while, however, just shuffling around. It might not be a person trapped inside after all.

"Maybe I should destroy whatever is in the bag," I said nervously. There was clearly something alive in it. Whatever it was, it knew that I was releasing it, it wasn't communicating and it might try to attack me. I thought about raising my sword in preparation to stab the bundle when I heard that familiar voice speak to me.

The voice of the Creator rang out in my ears. "Stand down. What is inside is very valuable."

I lowered the sword as he ordered. As soon as I did so, the top of the bundle began to open up.

I watched intently for whatever was about to come out. The opening widened to about six inches and then ten and then it opened even wider still. Out of the opening of the bag I saw what looked like wispy light grey hair.

If it was hair, there might be someone human inside. I looked to see if a weapon emerged, but nothing dangerous came out of the bag. I nonetheless kept my distance.

Next, a head appeared into view, naturally, attached to the hair. I could see it was the face of a petite old man with grey hair. His eyes were wide and wise, and were of a deep green hue. His skin was wizened and brown. His nose was pointed, narrow and long.

Finally, enough of the old man came out that I could see that he had his mouth covered with something. He was obviously unable to speak. This would explain why he never vocalized for help while stuck inside that bag! The old man's eyes pleaded to me for help. I immediately laid my sword down on the ground and reached towards the old man's mouth to help remove the gag that had been tied tightly around his head.

Once the leather cloth was removed, the man croaked out to me in a voice clearly strained from fatigue and struggle, "Thank you so much! You have saved my life! For that, I am eternally grateful!"

I didn't say anything in response because I was still surprised and not sure how to react.

The old man then whispered some words that I didn't understand. It sounded like "LeMe LeLease!"

CHAPTER NINE

After saying that incantation, the all ropes unwound and untied themselves and the blue linen bag fell away from him. Finally, I saw that his hair was all disheveled from being trapped in that bag and his clothes were tattered and singed.

"Who did this to you?" I asked him, wondering what kind of person would attack such an old man and what kind of motive they could have.

He looked at me intently with his deep green eyes as if he was about to say something. Before either of us could react or respond however, I got that twisting, sinking feeling again.

Suddenly, the old man and I were no longer in the same location. I was traveling again.

"Where am I going?" I asked myself. I was a little frustrated that I couldn't get more answers, but I wondered if I was going back to my world or someplace else that the old man was taking me. Even if I was going home, where and when would I be at home? My wandering thoughts didn't matter though; I couldn't see or hear anything while traveling. Everything was dark and fuzzy. I would soon find out where I would appear.

After a few moments, things around me began to brighten and clear, but I didn't recognize anything in front of me. At first, all I could see were flying colors and shapes. I squinted to see if I could recognize anything, but to no avail. Everything was warped and foggy. Gradually, the fog began to go away and as I looked, I began to realize where I was.

I was now in a classroom. A pencil was gripped in my fingers and my hands rested upon numerous sheets of papers and folders covered in my handwriting.

What school was this? How old was I? Where did I live now? I thought about these questions agitatedly, trying to remember the answers that must be somewhere in my mind.

The classroom was an old English style room. This was the first school I ever attended that had a cloakroom to keep coats. It secretly made me feel a little classy. However, it wasn't very cold yet, so the cloakroom wasn't getting much use today.

In this classroom were about thirty desks. Each desk had a work surface made of solid wood and the desk structure was made of iron with sturdy iron legs, all painted brown. These were much nicer than the cheap particle board desks I was used to from my previous schools. I sat in the middle of about four rows of seven to eight desks.

In the front of the class was a tall African American woman wearing wire framed glasses with thick lenses. Her face was elongated, accentuating her pointy cheekbones and chin, with big white teeth showing from her mouth. She looked a little dorky, but her voice was pleasant—soft when she spoke, yet still loud enough so that we could all hear. Her hair was black and tied back in a bushy ponytail. She wore a silky brown and orange dress that went down just below her knees. The dress fabric had a nice sheen under the lights, enough to look high-class, but not so shiny that it would be gaudy.

Looking around the room, I took note of all the other students in the classroom, studying their faces until I finally remembered where I was. I glanced down at my desk and I remembered that class was just finishing, so I was finalizing a few sentences on my notes before preparing to leave.

The instructor, Ms. Brown called out to the class genially, "All right, class. Put away your work; I know you're all so excited, but you can finish it at home!" She laughed at her little teacher joke.

I was so excited to get out of class. All of a sudden, in another wave of memories, I recalled I had safety patrol practice. I quickly put my work away into my school backpack and headed to the practice room. I automatically went out of the classroom, turned to the right and hurried for the stairs nearby. The stairwell was behind double doors painted green. The doors each had a reinforced plastic window in the middle and the paint around the door handles were chipped from every day wear and tear.

I was up on the third floor, so I had to run down two flights of stairs. The steps were made of concrete and had rough sandpaper-like strips along the edges of each step to make people less likely to slip. The stairwell walls were painted green to match the doors. Display cases hung on the walls, showing off various medals and plaques that different student teams had won throughout the years in competitions. I didn't have time to stop and look at them, but I could remember they varied from soccer to spelling or even chess. The photographs of proud groups of victorious students and teachers stared out the cases happily as I zoomed by them.

I descended the stairs two at a time, excited about practice. I burst through the double doors at the bottom. These doors opened up to the cafeteria: a very large room with long white tables lining up against the walls. To the left was the kitchen. The counters there were where you would get your food, sliding your lunch tray along, picking up your entrée, drink and sides. The safety patrol room was to the right through a single door on the other side of the white tables.

I went to the right towards the single green door. I didn't notice that there was someone lurking behind one of the tables by the door. I didn't know it at the time, but there was another 6th grader waiting for me there. His name was Jay, and he, on numerous occasions, would "accidentally" spill his lunch on me and trip me in gym or in the halls, just to name a few of his old tricks. Even fancy private schools had their share of jerks.

Jay was a few inches taller than me. He was thin and lanky with brown eyes and short spiky brown hair. Despite how scrawny he looked, he was a pretty wiry guy, and the fact that he was taller didn't help me any. Jay knew that I would be coming down to practice around this time. After all, lucky for me, he was in the safety patrol as well.

As I quickly approached the door, out of the corner of my eye, I noticed a blue sneaker attached to a tacky green sock. In a sudden rush of adrenaline as I realized in a split second the impending danger I was in, I stopped mid-stride and jerked myself to the side, just narrowly avoiding tripping over the out-stretched foot. My heart pounding after dodging Jay's attempt to trip me, I looked Jay in the eyes, in annoyance, to let him know that he was caught. This was the first time I had ever been able to evade this childish trick.

In response, Jay looked at me with a little surprise then snickered. He turned around and ran into the practice room without looking back. I waited a second, then came in after him, shaking my head from his stupidity.

When I walked in, there were ten other safety patrol students standing around near the walls. Some of them were putting on their reflective patrol uniforms, so I slipped mine on quickly too. Behind the table was Ms. Jackson, a petite bronzed woman. She had sparkling brown eyes, brown wavy hair with streaks of grey and she always wore a smile. The students loved her.

Safety was always Ms. Jackson's top priority, as she had seen many bad traffic accidents in the past. She was dedicated to the students and school, evident by her teaching this class for over twenty years. The safety patrol's job was to assist other students in safely crossing the streets, which was a valuable service in such an urbanized and busy city.

In a kind and clear voice, so that all in the room could hear, she announced that each student would stand at new positions around the school building for the upcoming parade, as the traffic flow would be different because of the event.

"Will all of you be able to attend the parade?" she asked. "I need all of you to take this form home to your parents and have them sign it." She walked by each student, handing each one a permission slip for volunteering at the school parade.

The form was a single sheet of paper that explained general information about the parade, like when and where the parade route would begin or end and what school departments were participating in it. There were blank lines at the bottom for the names and signatures of the student, parent, and teacher. I would have to get my mom to sign it when she got home from work.

"We will start practicing next week, every day after school. You can't come to practice until I get the form back signed by your parent, so remember to get it signed soon if you plan to attend," explained Ms. Jackson.

After hearing this, I became really excited. A parade! This would be the first parade I ever took part in! I only ever got to see parades on TV, so experiencing one in real life was something to look forward to. I thought about the upcoming event to myself eagerly, imagining colorful floats and balloons, dance troupes and flower arrangements, and marching bands in sequined costumes. Ms. Jackson explained more about the parade and what the safety patrol would do. I could hardly stay still in my seat as she talked.

While Ms. Jackson discussed more details, Jay and another student by the name of Willie, were not paying her any attention. Willie was around the same height as Jay. He had dark skin, an unkempt afro, large ears and mean little brown eyes. Jay and Willie were whispering as they occasionally gave me a foreboding look whenever the teacher was looking away from them. Even though I was focused on Mrs. Jackson and what she was saying, I could see them out of the corner of my eye. "What are those idiots planning?" I muttered inaudibly to myself.

After a few more moments of talking, Ms. Jackson told each person in the room which intersection they would be assigned to patrol. I would be working the corners of Bryant and R Streets along with students named Ricky, Rochelle, Regina and Matt. Our corners were in front of the school building. There were so many of us because the immediate front of the school had the most of the student traffic. After a few more words, she told everyone to head out to their respective corners because school was going to end soon.

Trying to give Jay as little time to prepare whatever harebrained scheme he was thinking of, I packed my things hurriedly and left the room, heading straight to my assigned corner. I wanted to avoid any possibility of dealing with Jay and his friend. I went out the door and turned left, going out the same way I had come into the practice room. When I crossed through the big cafeteria, I went out the green double doors and instead of going upstairs to where Ms. Brown's classroom was, I went directly straight into what was called the "main hall."

In the middle of the main hall, hanging from the ceiling was a large crystal chandelier—the centerpiece of the school lobby. It was over six feet in diameter, filled with sparkling Swarovski crystal glass hanging down over two feet from the high ceiling. All around the circumference of the chandelier were bright lights illuminating the huge hall. Golden chains adorned the chandelier structure, dangling alongside the thousands of twinkling crystals. For a long time, I didn't know if the glass crystals were made of real gemstones or not, until I'd asked a nice teacher at school who told me that they were made of a fancy glass. There was a plaque in the room that paid homage to the wealthy benefactor who had donated the fine chandelier to the school, hoping to "illuminate" the hearts and minds of the student body there.

Aside from housing the breath-taking lighting, this hall served as the main entrance of the school, and there were entries to stairwells leading up to the second floor on each side of the main hall. The administrative offices of the school were also found here.

After reaching the hall, I went under the chandelier, turned and headed towards the main entrance of the school. I ran, pushed the right double door open and raced outside, down the stairs, and to the sidewalk. The school grounds outside were flanked on each side by five foot high brick and mortar walls with fancy decorative posts and lamps about every forty feet and at every corner. Upon reaching the sidewalk, I turned left to get to my assigned position. I had just about reached my spot when the final school bell rang.

While running towards the corner of Bryant and R, I noticed my favorite person, Willie, standing on the north opposite corner, watching for me. I immediately wondered where Jay was. Just as the thought occurred in my mind, out of the corner of my left eye I noticed something near the ground, coming from behind a fence post just a few feet before me. I stopped running and with anger burning in my stomach, I took a few steps forward. Sure enough, hiding behind the corner of the brick wall was Jay with his leg ready to trip me. When Jay realized he was caught, after I stalked up, glaring at him, he ran like a weasel to his post down the street, with Willie tagging behind like a dumb dog. I was angry at them, but they weren't worth my time or even my breath. I had to get to work.

I continued to the corner I was supposed to man. I checked my clothes and uniform to make sure everything was as it should be. My safety patrol uniform was a bright neon yellow and orange rubber sash covered in a highly reflective coating. It was connected to a belt that went around my waist and the sash went over my right shoulder. Patrol students usually kept them in their backpacks and then put the uniform on over their normal school clothes when it was time for traffic duty.

I had reached my corner. The students from the school were coming out to the streets. I was ready to assist them. I would get to go home after about thirty minutes of patrol duty, since most of the kids would be well on their way home by then. A group of about twenty to thirty students came flooding out of the school, headed in my direction. They stopped at my corner, ready to cross the street to go home. I immediately stretched out my hands to stop the students from crossing the street as I saw that the appropriate traffic light across the street was about to turn red. The students stopped, and like clockwork, a stream of cars roared by noisily. The smell of gasoline and the sounds of honking horns, screeching brakes and revving engines filled the streets.

When the light turned green, I safely entered the crosswalk first to make sure the vehicles were all stopped before the students entered the crosswalk. The dozens of students crossed the street after waiting for me to lead. I stood in the middle of the street, next to fellow safety patrol student, Ricky, who was working the foot traffic from the other direction, most of parents coming to walk their kids home. We nodded at each other in greeting as we initially caught sight of each other.

I started heading back to the sidewalk after all of the students had crossed the street with Ricky and the light was about to turn red again. The cars waiting at their stop were ready to go as soon as their light turned green. My right foot had just reached the pavement with my left foot still on the asphalt when the cars once again began to impatiently rush by. While the cars wouldn't come close enough to hit me, they drove by close enough and fast enough, that they caused a strong gust of wind to rustle my clothes.

I met another large group of students at the sidewalk, waiting for their turn to go across the street. I stretched out my arm to signal the students from crossing the street while the light was red. I repeated what I did before. When our light turned green, I walked into the middle of the crosswalk before the others, leading them forward at an appropriate and safe time. This scenario occurred for about another twenty minutes.

After the last group of kids crossed the street, I headed back to the sidewalk. Virtually all of the students had left school. I then headed towards the school building. The other patrol students and I grabbed our backpacks from patrol class and said good bye to Ms. Jackson for the day.

As I walked south away from the school building, I realized that the pranksters were no longer around. I surveyed the area, but I couldn't spot them anywhere, so I figured they had ditched traffic patrol early and gone home to goof off. It was time that I walk towards home, finally able to relax now that I was off duty and those annoying boys were gone. I was happy thinking about the parade coming up and felt good after doing a helpful community service like safety patrol.

I watched other schoolmates walking home with their parents or friends, or heading to a fast food place to get an after school meal. Pigeons pecked away on sidewalks nearby, scavenging on tidbits left behind by the eating kids. Just as I was enjoying this simple scenery, all of a sudden my body jerked forward violently.

It wasn't anything that I had done. I hadn't tripped on anything either. My stomach clenched. Before my eyes were visions of a big house that I didn't really recognize and the swirling of the familiar colors of purple and gold. It made me feel kind of sick. I needed to get home, and quickly. I was too dizzy to run back, so I thrust my hands into my pockets, clutching the gem in one hand, and tried to start powerwalking home awkwardly.

While seeing these visions, I wasn't fully aware of where I was going, but I was still walking in the right direction thanks to my motor memory. I couldn't focus or see well, but I managed to get by all the street crossings without incidence. If Ms. Jackson could see me stumbling around the streets right now, she'd have a fit!

I fought the dizziness and disorienting flashes for many minutes, taking it easy, moving ahead steadily, step by step. I was only a block away from home when the visions finally stopped. At last, I had a clear enough head to start thinking about what was even waiting for me at home.

When I remembered what it was my heart sunk into my guts.

It was him. My brother's father was there at home—Bernard...

Bernard was never any fun to be around and he was much worse when he was drunk, which unfortunately, was quite often. He was loud, angry, and when drunk, he was prone to using his fists—even against my mom, as I had seen and heard firsthand a few times. While she must have had reasons to date him long ago, I couldn't imagine that any of those qualities my mother saw in him before were still there. I was legitimately scared of him and I knew that even though my mom would never admit it to me, she was scared of him too.

He was probably at the house, drinking and smoking my mom's hard-earned cash away on the sofa, like the no-good, lazy bum he was. My mother, meanwhile, was still at work. My brother hardly ever came home until late in the evening, after hanging out with his friends all day. I couldn't blame him for that though; no one would want to come home to that drunken slob. Unfortunately, this meant that I had to come home alone to Bernard often.

As I kept walking, I felt a little bad for my little brother, and suddenly felt a little guilty about how I had shunned him in the past, when we were living with Georgia and Wes. I myself didn't have a father, but at least I didn't have one that leeched on the family or abused us. It was no wonder that Darius was always out of the house with his friends; he had no one that he could trust to come home to. I realized then that the two of us weren't so different after all, despite how we'd grown apart.

I had now reached the front of my apartment building. This was a six story, red brick building. The shape was boring—a rectangle set with repetitive square windows, entirely devoid of any creativity or charm. Still, it was housing that my mother could afford with her own income, since Bernard was unemployed. It was also in a better neighborhood than our last apartment, plus it was very close to a really good elementary school. My mom did her best choosing with this apartment, but I couldn't say the same for her choosing Bernard.

Before heading up the cement stairs to the front door, I stopped and wondered what I would have to face when I got home. I sighed, looking at the ground, thinking about what trouble might happen if Bernard was in a foul mood. There was nothing I could really do. I shrugged it off and started to slowly go up the stairs. I knew I had to go home, but I definitely took my time doing it.

When I reached the top of the stairs, I inserted the apartment building's front door key into the big outer gate door. It served as a barrier against strangers who might otherwise wander around the apartment complex, causing trouble. I turned the key to the right, then turned the knob and pushed the gate open.

In front of me were the stairs that led up to my home. As I climbed the stairs, I thought about what Bernard would do or say to me. Was he angry and drunk? Was he going to be loud and violent? I was too tired and too worried to even think about the pyramid gem in my pocket. These anxious thoughts penetrated my mind while climbing the stairs to the third floor to my apartment.

I soon reached apartment number 310, where I lived. The door had the numbers screwed in above a small, round, glass peep hole. Above the knob was a metal bolt lock which was very thick. I walked softly to the front door and placed my left ear against the surface, hoping I wouldn't hear Bernard walking around or watching TV inside.

I didn't hear anything coming from within my apartment after several moments, so I breathed a sigh of relief to myself, saying, "Maybe he isn't home after all." It was also possible that he was passed out or napping.

So I took out my key ring and after finding the right key—a medium sized brass one engraved with the key company's logo—I inserted the brass key into the key hole, turning it clockwise slowly. I could hear the bolt unlock. I held my breath. The sound of the bolt was always loud, no matter how slowly I tried to unlock the door. I reluctantly pushed the door open.

It opened with a creaking sound. The reek of old cigarette smoke and musk from within assaulted my nostrils. Inside the apartment were tables, chairs and a three-seat sofa. On the right side of the room was a flat screen television with a twenty inch screen. The TV was surrounded by small statues and trophies, dusty remnants of Bernard's past glory as a college football player.

An octagonal coffee table sat between the television and the couch. On the dark plywood table was an ashtray full of cigarette butts and messily scattered ashes. Bernard usually smoked indoors because he was too lazy and inconsiderate to move a few feet to the balcony or outside. It was a non-smoking apartment too; the landlord would have a fit if he ever smelled what Bernard had done to the place.

The dining area was towards the back of the room, continuous with the living room area. We had a round plastic dining table with four chairs; the set of dining furniture had periwinkle surfaces and iron legs painted black. The legs of one of the chairs were slightly bent from a time Bernard had thrown some inebriated temper tantrum. No one was in the house as far as I could see.

Then I heard a voice coming from one of the bedrooms. The sudden sound made me jump and cringe.

"Lorenzo," Bernard grumbled loudly. "Did you take out the trash?" He never said hello to me or asked me how my day was.

I immediately went to the kitchenette to get the trash out of the plastic garbage pail. The kitchen was very small. Yellow floral wallpaper covered the walls. A stove with an electric cooktop sat in the corner, near a window with pretty red curtains that my mom had bought and put up. To the left of the window was a scratched porcelain sink and white plastic counter. By the counter was a white re-frigerator standing about six feet tall, covered in magnets and note paper scribbled with groceries and to-do lists. A cream-colored cordless phone hung on the wall beside the fridge. A few feet away from the phone was the entrance to the other part of the apartment—the bedrooms, from where Bernard was talking to me, probably collapsed in bed, drunk as a skunk.

I put my backpack down by the foot of the sofa, got a new trash bag from the cabinet under the sink, pulled out the full trash bag and tied it up, holding my breath to avoid the stench of old food scraps, and put it to the side. After putting in the fresh new trash bag, I grabbed the old trash by the knot on top and carried towards the front door. I was just about to leave with the garbage when Bernard suddenly appeared.

Standing at about six feet and two inches, with a furious expression atop his broad shoulders and muscular frame, he looked absolutely frightening. He had black, tightly curled hair and his eyes were dark and cheerless. My blood ran cold at the sight of him.

In a very aggravated tone, he shouted at me, "Didn't I tell you take out the trash!? Why's you takin' so long!?"

I stood looking at him silently in immense fear with the garbage bag still clenched tightly in my hand. I could smell the cheap booze on his breath as he hollered at me, slurring and spraying me with flecks of beer-scented saliva.

When Bernard finally saw that I was already holding the trash, he said to me impatiently, "Well! Don't just stand there like an idiot! Get it done!!"

As I walked by him, keeping my eyes averted and shoulders and head lowered in submission, he raised his right hand and smacked me in the back of the head—hard.

My head jerked forward, darkness and stars flashed before my eyes, and my skin stung from the blow. A little dizzy and furious from the unnecessary shouting and the slap, I walked a little faster towards the front door, quickly grabbing the knob and going outside into the hall. When I got outside, I headed for the stairs. I had to go to the first floor to get to the communal dumpster. The front door closed loudly behind me. I didn't realize how hard I had shut the door.

While starting down the stairs, I heard Bernard yelling hysterically, muffled behind the door, "Boy!! You wait 'til you get back, slamming that door at me!!" He kept screaming and cursing at me from within the room and threatening what he'd do to me when I got back.

I picked up the pace going down the stairs. How I wished I could be away from this man. He was far worse than my Aunt Georgia; she never got drunk and hit me. He was even worse than any school bully; I at least didn't have to live with Jay or Willie, or have to watch them abuse both me and my family!

I finally reached the bottom floor. I turned left and headed towards the back of the building where the dumpsters were. On the way, I walked by two apartments with damaged doors that had marks from being punched or hung slightly askew on crooked hinges. I smelled more smoke and trash and also heard other people yelling and cussing from inside the apartments. I was used to this. I just kept walking and blocked it out.

When I arrived at the back door of the apartment complex, I opened it and headed to the big metal dumpster. The lid was left open as usual, making it easy for people to throw their trash in. It looked like someone had gone through the dumpster earlier, as pieces of garbage littered the ground around it. It was probably a tenant, scouring the garbage for recyclables.

I picked up the trash bag and tossed it into the bin and headed back towards the iron back door.

"Is there anything I can do to make things better?" I asked myself sadly.

Telling Mom wouldn't make any difference. I had complained to her about him plenty of times before and she was no fool. She knew the bruises he left. If I were older, if I were a man, I'd kill him the next time he ever put his hands on me or her—even if it meant going to jail. I groaned to myself as I slumped against the building's back wall. No, that wasn't a good idea! I couldn't do that!

Tears started to well up in my eyes as I thought about my real father, who had left us. Where was my dad? Why did he leave us when I was only two? Why couldn't he come back now to help us? These thoughts bubbled in my mind as I turned the knob to open the back door and reentered the apartment building.

I took my time walking back down the hall and back up the stairs, not wanting to face Bernard, hoping he'd downed a few more beers while I was gone and forgotten everything. Once I got to the apartment door, I listened at the door for any sounds of movement. All I heard was noise from the television. He was in the living room.

I turned the knob slowly. As soon as I had opened the door a few inches though, Bernard shouted, "Git in here!!"

Once I was inside, even before the door could close, he yelled at me while sitting on the couch, "How many times do I have to tell you not to slam the door?!"

Actually, I had only ever slammed the door on purpose once and I never did it again. The rest of the times he'd claimed I did it were just in his head. Still, there was no point in arguing with him. I said nothing and just looked down towards the floor, which he had by now dropped a crinkled beer can onto.

"What took you so long!?" Spit flew from his mouth as he kept shouting.

I had no words to say to him. I just kept looking down at my feet as he shouted.

"Boy! You listenin' to me?!"

Without any warning, the gem in my pocket started glowing and buzzing.

"What the hell is that?!" Bernard looked a little surprised. "Your ma gave you a cell phone? She never gave me no cell! Give it to me, boy!"

I couldn't give him the gem! I started to panic. What was I going to do? I started to back away from him.

"Give it to me now!!" Bernard's voice was louder, if that was even possible. He was getting up from the couch, sweaty and heaving, and glared at me with narrowed bloodshot eyes. "I'm not going to say it again," he threatened, raising his arm menacingly.

I backed up faster. I was about to run to the front door, in desperate attempt to keep the gem away from him, when I felt that familiar queasy feeling. I realized that I was now moving, but didn't know where. I was relieved that I had escaped something terrible, and hoped my real world self would be okay next time I saw it.

CHAPTER TEN

The spinning continued for what seemed like forever. It definitely lasted longer than all the other times. After a few moments, I tried to open my eyes and the blackness began to dissipate. My eyes slowly adjusted to the new surroundings. Like the last time I had entered, I seemed to have landed on my feet just fine.

So I stood up, eyes not yet completely clear, but clear enough to recognize that I was in the same room that I had left last time. Bernard was gone. Instead, in front of me was the little old man that I had rescued. He had been gagged and tied up in a sack behind a blockaded door in a destroyed room of his strange mansion before I got him out.

I was finally able to talk to him. I asked him, "What is your name?"

"I am Thiek, son of Yenirb. And what is your name, young man?" he asked in return. He smoothed out his clothes and long grey hair as he asked, trying to make himself look more presentable.

"My name is Lorenz."

"Lorenz, son of whom?" asked Thiek expectantly.

"Son of Yorgreg." The name just flew out of my mouth. It felt somehow felt natural, so I tried not to question it.

Thiek wore a torn shirt decorated with black feathers and bronzed leather shorts made of tough hide. Even though his clothing was damaged, his body was in good shape. No scars or cuts or bruises marred his flesh. I was surprised since Nathanu had told me that the man who lived in the grey house on the hill was dead. Apparently he'd thought the old man had died while tied up in the bag.

There had to be something special about this man. I remembered how after Thiek had uttered some kind of incantation, the ropes just came right off him. He must have great powers.

Thiek saw that I was brimming with questions and curiosity. He told me in a comforting voice, "In time, many questions will be answered. One must be patient, Lorenz."

I nodded. I decided to ask him the straightforward question first. "How did you end up trapped in this bag?" I motioned towards the blue linen sack now discarded on the floor.

"There was a group of treacherous robbers that surprised me," Thiek replied. "They had been watching me for some time and had learned about some of my powers and studied my daily habits. They snuck inside and ambushed me all at once while I was busy studying in the room. One of them had stolen some of the control powder to subdue me while I fended myself from the other two."

While listening to him, I remembered when Jbug and his crew tried to subdue and rob me too. Thiek saw from my facial expression that I seemed to recognize the bandits he mentioned.

He asked me, "Do you know these robbers?"

"No, not really, but I've …seen them before." My brows furrowed and lip curled in distaste. My encounter with the trio was far too close and thoughts of that night still caused anger and adrenaline to well up.

"It's no matter," said Thiek. "Men such as those criminals will eventually get what is coming to them. A life of evil will never reward one with rich fruit."

I was silent, lost in thought, my fists clenched.

The old man saw that I was feeling upset and tried to lighten up the mood. "Lorenz, son of Yorgreg! You are welcome in my home anytime! Please, let us get something to eat! I'm famished after being tied up so long!" said Thiek heartily. "Please allow me to lavish my savior with my finest food and drink!"

He extended his hand, inviting me to leave the chamber and head out into the hallway to make our way to the dining room. I was all for a good meal, so I headed over to the door and held it open for him.

Thiek thanked me as he went through the door. I followed behind him. He turned into the hallway, and after looking back to make sure I was keeping up, began to descend the stairs. "This way," he said.

"This is a really large house!" I stated, trying to make friendly conversation. "It's very beautiful."

"Yes, I have been here a long, long time. This home has been in my family for many generations." Thiek gestured towards the numerous smiling portraits of his ancestors on the walls. "My family has helped countless people of all races. We have always been good benefactors in our community. There is good and there is evil in the world, and we have always tried to live by the right way."

When I heard that last sentence, I stopped in mid-stride at the bottom of the stairs. It sounded just like what the Creator had told me in the tree hollow.

Thiek had just reached the door to the dining room when he realized I was standing stock still on the steps. He turned around and said me with thick sincerity, "Come, lad! I'm not going to harm you. You are safe! Certainly much safer than you were with those men that attempted to rob you."

I stared at him. How could he have known that? I didn't tell him that Jbug and his companions had tried to rob me. This aroused a mixture of curiosity and suspicion in me, but I just followed him through the dining room door quietly.

We wound up in a large kitchen with numerous cabinets all around. There were two large, wood-burning iron stoves next to each other to my right. In the middle of the room was a large rectangular table with a matching set of wooden chairs around it. Next to one of the stoves was an eight foot tall oval hole in the wall. From where I was standing, I couldn't see inside of it.

Thiek directed me to have a seat in one of the wooden chairs. I took off my heavy backpack and chose to sit in the first chair to my left at one end of the table.

The old man, gesturing to his torn and dirty shirt and shorts, then took the chance to tell me, "Please excuse me, good Lorenz. I'm sorry, but I must get a change of clothing before I do anything else."

I agreed and he thanked me again. At the end of the table was another door that led out of the kitchen and into another part of the house. As soon as he disappeared through the doorway, I began to assess the entire room with my eyes.

A tall cabinet stood behind me, over seven feet high and three feet wide. Presumably, cookware and food were stored inside. To the left of the cabinet were many large shelves filled with books of all sorts of colors and sizes, and shelves full of cooking utensils and supplies.

I was intrigued by the books that were on the shelves. I was too far away to read the spines of the books well, so I slid back in my chair, ready to get up when the door opened up again.

Thiek was back. He was now dressed in a purple, yellow and white robe. The material looked like thick, luxurious wool, accented with bright dyes and silk sashes. I had never seen robes anything like it.

As if reading my thoughts, he grinned to me cheerily. "Oh, so you like this robe! It's just a little different, but in a good way!"

After having a laugh, Thiek went to the cupboard and pulled out some grapes, figs, bread, cheese and various exotic fruits. He placed the food in a wooden bowl and carried it over to the table for us to eat. I grabbed a small loaf of bread from the bowl and started to chew on it ravenously. I was hungry! I just didn't realize how hungry I was. All the excitement had really taken it out of me.

I picked up one of the fruits I didn't recognize. The fruit was yellow and rounded, and shaped like a giant bean. The skin was very fragrant and thin, and the peel was covered in red speckles. When I bit into the flesh, I found it was very soft, sweet and juicy. I really enjoyed the taste of the fruit, which I had never experienced before. Before I knew it, I had eaten three in a few minutes, leaving the large fibrous pits of the fruits discarded on the table. I didn't say very much while eating because I was too busy filling my stomach with the delicious, refreshing food.

After letting me eat undisturbed for several minutes, Thiek got up from the chair across from me and went to one of the shelves. He picked up a thick blue book and then returned to his seat and grabbed a fig.

I looked at the book and after wiping some of the sticky juice away from my mouth and licking my lips, I asked him, "What is that book about?"

"It's about something that is very special—something I believe you were chosen to do."

"What is that?"

He looked solemnly at the book and then at me. "It is a book of cigam—knowledge that gives you the power to change, to create, to destroy, to heal and to do many other great things."

My eyes widened in disbelief and shock.

"With such power also comes much responsibility," said Thiek gravely. "Such power can take control of you, making you a different person. If you are not firm of heart... it can turn you into a monster."

I listened intently. I stopped eating and watched him silently, showing him that I was giving him my full attention.

"If you are not careful, you could become a terrible creature like Davian—one who is feared in all the land."

I didn't know who or what Davian was, but it sounded scary. I hoped that I wouldn't have to meet this creature in my travels.

Thiek continued his speech, looking me straight in the eyes as he spoke. "For this great power you must have sincere commitment and work tirelessly, and you will also be exposed to very much danger."

I wondered to myself if it was worth this much trouble just for power. What was this power even, anyways? I didn't know a thing about it or this strange land.

Thiek then slid the book over to me across the tabletop. "Is this what you want?"

I didn't respond. I was still thinking about everything he had just said. Suddenly, the bowl of food on the table began to rise several inches off the surface. I leaned back into my chair in amazement. I looked to the ceiling to see if a string were pulling up the bowl. I also turned and bent my head closer to the table to look under the bowl. Nothing physical was holding or pushing the bowl up. It was genuinely floating! I then looked at Thiek, noticing that his lips were moving slightly, as if he were uttering something silently.

"What is this? How did you do that?" I asked.

"It's cigam." The old man said with a satisfied smirk. "I can teach you to be very good." The bowl then returned to the table.

"I don't know…" I murmured hesitantly.

Thiek watched my expressions intently, trying to read me. He secretly hoped that I would say yes. He wanted someone to carry on his family's cigam legacy and he needed to train someone to be able to stand up to the evil Davian.

Inside, I knew this was what I needed to do. Maybe this choice was what the voice was preparing me for. That familiar feeling told me to accept Thiek's offer, but how could I be sure it really was the right choice and I wasn't just being used? I was confused and didn't know which way to go. The last time I had trusted someone, I had fallen into a foolish trap. Then, I thought about the voice in the forest and how he had told me to find someone. I thought about how Thiek or his cigam might help me complete this task.

I made my decision. I took the book from him.

Thiek smiled as I started looking through the pages. "This is just one of the many books you will use as you learn."

I didn't respond. I could only think about so much at once, and right now I was focusing on the first page. It was a creamy color with dark writing. The page was titled "The Naicigam's Master." The next page had a long list of strange words. I stared at the foreign words, puzzled.

Thiek immediately noticed my confusion and said, "These are skills and spells that you can learn to cast. It also gives general information about each spell, like what it does and how long it lasts. There are also all of the ingredients that are required to make the potions for the spell to work."

I went through a few more pages. After I had looked through many of the pages, I closed the book and placed it in my bag.

Happy to see me consent to learning cigam from him, Thiek decided that it would be good for me to get the components for my first spell.

I finished off the last of the food that I had grabbed from the bowl and told him okay.

If I could learn spells anything like what he used to levitate the bowl, I definitely wanted to learn how to use this cigam.

"So, what tools or weapons do you have?" asked Thiek.

"Three swords and a shield," I replied. "Do I need something else?"

"Ah yes, you will need something special to help you use these spells." He nodded, smiling.

"What?" I asked.

"A wand," he said. "It helps the cigam work. Without a wand, you won't be able to use some cigam spells."

"Wow, where do I get this wand?" I wondered if I'd have to buy one somewhere.

"I have an extra one somewhere in the house that you can have. It is the least I can do for you," Thiek answered assuredly.

I was excited to have a wand to go along with the stuff I already had. If I could learn things like telekinetically lifting a bowl, what else would I be able to do?

Excitedly, I got up out of my chair and followed Thiek as he headed back to through the door into the main room. We got to the stairs and started climbing to the second floor. I would have been racing up the steps two at a time if I weren't trying to control myself and follow after him respectfully.

Thiek continued to explain to me, "Remember, you have to study to learn how to use these tools. If you use them before you are ready, it will not do what you want it to do. Studying is important. There is thought behind every action."

I nodded in confirmation.

By the time he had finished what he was saying, we were at the top of the stairs. This time, instead of turning into the hallway where I had found the room Thiek was in, he led me into the other hall. Initially it was dark, but when he held out his hand, the candelabra all along the halls lit up with an audible whoosh. He continued down the hall for about twenty feet and then stopped at a door on the left.

After stopping, he stood directly in front of the door. He tapped the door three times towards each corner of the door, beginning with the top left and then circling clockwise to the others.

I wondered what he was doing. Maybe this door was locked in some special way to protect the contents from people like Jbug, like some kind of big magical safe.

After knocking on the door, I heard the door latch click and the door swung itself open gently. There was no light coming from the new room initially. Thiek then stepped inside the door and then, as I had grown to expect, the candlesticks in the room ignited dramatically.

He looked around the room and turned to see that I was by the door. When he saw I was there, he told me to be careful not to touch anything. I stood back a few feet from Thiek, letting him do his work.

There were a great many different things in this room, including large padlocked chests, a long wooden bookcase laden with tomes and glass bottles filled with dried herbs, and three doors along the three walls.

The chests were all made of plated iron with generous bands of gold following the contours. They looked expensive and valuable on their own, but were far too large and heavy for a burglar to carry away. For extra safeguarding, chained to each chest was a huge padlock. I noticed that the uniformly-sized chests were big enough to be used as a makeshift coffin for even a large adult. I shook this morbid thought out of my head, telling myself that everything would be okay and not to think of such things.

Thiek looked around the room and then said, "This must be where it is." He was facing the large bookcase. He reached into the third shelf from the bottom, into the right corner, stretching his arm behind some books that were on the shelf there. When he pulled back his arm, he was holding a narrow grey rod about twenty inches long.

I was initially a little disappointed with the appearance of the wand. It was just a plain stick. I knew not to judge a book by its cover, though.

After pulling it out, he whirled around and showed the wand to me, exclaiming, "This is it! This is what you will need to work your cigam. It will help you fight many dangers and great evil."

"Danger and great evil…?"

"Yes, great evil like Davian or Nireficul. They have ways of persuading people, and came into power through convincing others—particularly cigamians—to trust them. He takes not only their powers, but their confidence and belief in themselves. You must avoid this evil for now, until you are ready for him. They will be very difficult to defeat. Many have tried and failed, claiming them to be indomitable, but I believe it is possible to stop them. Not with strength only, but with knowledge, the power of cigam and the belief in oneself."

I didn't understand all of what I had heard, but it was clear that some bad people were out there and that I might have to one day face and defeat them.

Thiek saw potential in me. He believed that I could do it. He smiled and with both hands, he handed me the wand. He carried it with the tip facing the ceiling, kind of like how you might hand someone a sharp knife or a gun.

He went on to say, "This wand was once owned by a very special friend and powerful cigam-user."

I grabbed the wand with my right hand, closing my fingers all around it. All of a sudden I felt this immense rush. It was like a refreshing spring breeze just blew past me, but nothing else in the room moved. "Did you feel that?" I asked Thiek.

"No. What you felt was probably the wand accepting you as its new owner. Each wand is unique and will work best if it is compatible with the soul of its wielder. Does it feel all right?"

"Yeah!" I was so excited I wanted to try a trick immediately, but didn't have the first clue as to what to do. "Uh… What can I do with this?" I asked Thiek.

He stroked his chin while contemplating my question. "Let's see…" He pointed at a stray book lying on the ground. "I can do this without the help of a wand, but you will need to use one for now. Think about that book over there near the wall. Point your wand directly at it. Picture it rising."

I did exactly as he told me. I concentrated as hard as I could on the little leather-bound book. At first nothing happened. After a minute or so of trying without any success, I began to wonder if it just wasn't going to work. I didn't know what to do different; I was trying so hard already!

Then all of a sudden, I saw something move. Were my eyes playing tricks on me? The book jiggled a little and then it seemed to rattle up off the ground an inch or so. My eyes widened, realizing I had actually done cigam! I tried to bring it higher in the air and the book complied, floating up several more inches. It wavered unsteadily, but stayed hovering. This was too cool. I looked back at Thiek.

He had a smile on his face. "Excellent! I knew you would be a natural at this. Now, don't drop it. Try to gently place it back onto the floor."

I imagined the book being lowered to the floor. It landed slowly and safely. After setting it down, I turned to face Thiek to see what was next.

"Good. Now, the first thing I need you to do is to start reading your cigam book. I will show you to your room. You can use this room to rest and study your first spells."

I was glad that he was taking me to my room because I was dead tired. It had actually been a long day. I had been distracted from my sleepiness all day, asking him questions, talking about evil creatures, and being excited about cigam. Now that he mentioned rest, I could feel the weariness creeping up on me.

So we left the room and continued down the hallway. As we passed some of the closed doors, I asked Thiek what was in the rooms. He told me that they were filled with various books and items that he needed for spell work. and that if I was also a dedicated cigamian, I would eventually accrue as many things as well.

After we had gone forward for a while and crossed most of the hall, Thiek extended his hand and snapped his fingers. Candlesticks on the walls suddenly lit up a staircase that spiraled downstairs. This staircase was not as wide as the other one down the hall and it wasn't the same color. Unlike the opulently decorated main stairway covered in gold and royal purples, this modest staircase was made of a simple dark wood. The steps had round circular designs carved into them.

As we descended, I saw burning candles in bronze sconces along the walls. They were shaped like dragon heads with the candlelight glowing from their mouths.

At the bottom of the wooden staircase were two doors. One was directly in front and one was to the left. Thiek went towards the door to the left.

"Here it is, Lorenz." He turned the square knob, knocked on the top right of the door and it swung open inward.

He stepped in and I followed. My eyes widened with amazement as I looked around the room. The rounded ceiling was filled with a glowing sea of stars. It was like the night sky if you could see the entire galaxy.

The walls were all painted with two enormous dragons, every detail so perfectly placed, that the dragons looked as if they were real. They were facing each other—one red and the other blue. The red one had flames bursting from its mouth and the other spewed out a blue liquid that might be water. The fire and water met each other with an incredible cloud of steam that coiled around their legs and feet.

In the middle of the room was a large four-post bed with an iron frame and headboard. It was immaculately made and topped with a quilted blanket with an embroidered dragon motif, neatly drawn up over plush pillows. All along the walls ran long wooden benches. At the foot of the bed was a chest with blankets, towels and clothes piled on top, ready for use.

"This is your room," Thiek said finally, after letting me soak the scenery in.

"What is all this, Thiek?" I asked him with awe.

"This room is called the 'soul room.' This chamber represents the soul of the one staying in it." He nodded approvingly while he admired the artwork.

"My soul is full of dragons?"

"No, but your soul is strong like the dragons." He chuckled at my question. "The heart of the dragons will protect you. No more questions for now, Lorenz. You must rest so you can begin your study."

I'm in a soul room and dragon hearts will protect me? I tried to figure out what all this meant. I was still in awe.

Thiek patted me on the back. "Prepare yourself to retire for the night, lad. I will fetch you your belongings from the dining room." He started to walk out of the chamber.

I suddenly jumped up. "Wait! I can get them!"

"No, you need your rest. Get comfortable with your new surroundings. You have an even longer day tomorrow. I am not going to take your belongings. You still do not trust me?" The old man spoke softly and soothingly.

His frank words stung when I realized that he was right. I lowered my gaze in embarrassment. There was no reason for me to doubt him. I had saved his life after all, which he was very thankful for. He also had been very hospitable to me, giving me food and a nice place to live. He was even teaching me magic spells with my own wand and spell book!

Nevertheless, deep inside, something told me not to trust him completely. It was true. Anything was possible. The last man whom I had trusted had also given me food and a place to stay, but then he had tried to kill me in my sleep. My intuition told me that I could trust that Thiek wouldn't take any of my belongings, though.

With that, Thiek left the room and I heard him walk away. After I couldn't hear his footsteps anymore, I started to get ready for bed. I took off my boots and suit. I hoped that I would get to wash them soon. They were dirty from all the dusty, sweaty traveling.

The floor around the bed was richly carpeted and felt good on my bare feet. I pulled out a spare set of clothes, from the pile on the trunk by the foot of the bed, to use as sleepwear.

After putting it on, I pulled back the comforter that had the green dragon on it. Underneath was a nice satiny sheet that looked really inviting. By now, I could barely hold my eyes open. Needless to say, I crawled under the comfy covers with great relish. As soon as I laid my head down on the fluffy pillows, my eyes closed and I was asleep.

CHAPTER ELEVEN

When my eyes slowly opened the next morning, I felt excited thinking about what might happen today. After a few moments and a few blinks, I started to realize that was something was different.

Where was I? Did Thiek send me someplace? I knew I shouldn't have trusted him!

I jumped out of bed hastily, forcefully throwing off my covers, and... saw that I was in a normal room in the real world.

It was a completely normal bedroom. No dragons or stars or fancy downy quilts. The bed I was sleeping on was a small creaky spring mattress tucked against the corner by a window with horizontal window blinds. The walls were all plain and beige. I glanced around and found there was a full length mirror and nearby was a wooden dresser undoubtedly full of my clothes.

As I continued to observe the room, I began to remember, in little bits and pieces, that I was in my mother's home. I was now in the real world. I had no idea of what day or time it was. It was light outside. On the dresser, amongst some grooming supplies, an alarm clock with glowing red digital numbers told me that it was currently 7:25 in the morning. I didn't have a calendar in my room though, so I still didn't know what day it was.

I left my bedroom and saw a stove, cabinets and refrigerator. I had wandered into the kitchen. To my left I saw a sliding glass door to the backyard. Out of sight somewhere outside, my mom's new dog was barking at something, probably a squirrel.

I faced the living room now, which was adjacent to the kitchen. Past the sofa and little flat screen TV, in a small hallway, was an open door. It was the bathroom. I took a step towards the bathroom, thinking I could refresh myself at the sink and try to remember my current living situation.

Then a woman's voice rang out, "Lorenzo, sleepy-head, you've gotta get ready to go to school!" It was the lovely voice of my mother! "I've got breakfast ready, and Darius already left! You better step it up, honey, or you'll be late!"

"I'm up! Don't worry!" Smiling to myself, I hurried into the bathroom to wash up.

After brushing, taking a quick shower and getting dressed, I went into the kitchen, which smelled wonderful. My mom had made us a hearty breakfast, and had already set it on the dining table. In front of my seat, there was a delicious-looking plate of scrambled eggs and crispy bacon, with fork and napkin on the side.

I sat down and ate it with gusto. It was great to taste my mom's cooking again. Meanwhile, Mom had already finished her meal and was on her way to work. She had gotten a full-time job recently as a bank teller, and was dressed sharply in a crisp burgundy power suit and heels, with her hair neatly clipped back.

"Make sure you clean up the house after school! Love you!" she called to me as she left the front door, swallowing the last of her eggs and bacon and tossing the dirty dishes in the dishwasher.

I told her that I would. Cleaning up the house typically consisted of vacuuming, doing the dishes, and taking out the trash. I hardly even caught sight of her in all the hustle and bustle of the weekday morning and she was always so busy between work and housework that we didn't get to spend much free time together. I would always help her out with the chores if I could. It was the least I could do for her. I finished my breakfast, put the plate and fork in the dishwasher and got ready to leave for school.

It was a different school, since we now lived in a new place, away from Bernard. Mom had finally decided to split up with him, and things had been much easier since.

This time, my was about five blocks away. I was still in the 6th grade, but now the school year was almost over. There was only about a month left until summer vacation. It wasn't as nice as my last school and it certainly wasn't my favorite either. I had only been going here for a few weeks and there were already a few students that loved to torment me here.

Unfortunately, one of them lived only two blocks away from my house on route to school. His name was Tony and he was a big guy about six feet tall. I usually tried to detour around his house, while on the way to school, to avoid him. I went left before the block with his house, up the side street a ways and eventually turned right to get back on track for the rest of the stretch to school. Today, the only people I saw outside were a few schoolmates who I wasn't familiar with. When I didn't see him, I felt a little sigh of relief.

I had not even walked a half block when I heard that voice behind me.

"Lorenzo, wait up," shouted Tony in his commanding tone.

An anxious knot forming in the pit of my stomach, I stopped and reluctantly turned around. I didn't want to, but I did. I pretended to be somewhat excited to see him. "Hey, Tony. What's up?"

"You got a dollar?" he asked.

"Nah, I don't." I replied, shrugging my shoulders.

"Yes you do; you always got money," he argued.

"No, I didn't get any allowance today, man."

"Gimme a dollar, man!"

"I said I don't have one!"

He was now inches away from me, towering over me by nearly a foot. Despite his intimidating stature, it was weird. For a brief second, I noticed that the fear and anxiety I experienced a few moments ago had gone. I stood erect, prepared for whatever he might do. I wondered to myself where this boldness was coming from, but I already knew the answer.

Tony moved closer to me, letting me know he was serious. I looked back at him intensely, letting him know that I wasn't going to back down. Strangely enough, Tony then cracked a half smile, and reached towards me to pat me on the shoulder.

I took a step back, moving my shoulder away from him, and he simply said to me, "See ya at school, dude." And just like that, he walked off.

I was totally amazed. What just happened? What did I do? Whatever it was, I was glad that I didn't make him angry and get beat up or lose my money. I had ended up giving my pocket change or lunch money to him so many times before. But today, he just let me go. Maybe in the end, all I'd needed was some confidence.

I continued my walk intentionally slowly until Tony had made it several houses away from me. I wanted to give him a head start so that I could walk the rest of the way to school with him far away from me, in case he got any new ideas.

On each side of the street were brick houses of different colors. Most had wooden porches out front with a bench or swing. Some houses had my favorite combination of the two—a swinging bench. Those were always fun to goof around on with friends, which I'd done plenty of times since moving here, since Mom would always let me go out to play after I'd finish my homework.

Cars of various makes, models and colors zoomed by. Some were headed to school or to work, or to wherever. Sometimes I'd guess where the people inside might be going, to pass the time while walking. Given that the blue sedan that just hurried past me had two classmates sitting inside, I'd wager that one was heading to my school.

Visible in the skyline, down the cross street, was a huge round white building. That was the stadium, where the city held its sports games and music concerts. The area would be absolutely packed full of people and cars during a football game or if a big singer came to town. My mom had taken me to a game there once for my birthday. The air was so abuzz with excitement and the roars of cheering fans. It was quite the experience.

I was almost at the school now, a large brick building with white posts and columns. It was only a block away and I could see the school's electric billboard flashing advertisements or notices out to students and parents about the school's sports teams and the dates of the upcoming summer break.

There were a number of other students streaming into the school as well, arriving from their parents' cars, or via bus, by bike, or on foot. I recognized some of them and didn't recognize others. As I got closer, I began to dread being there.

There were so many students that were just cruel people who liked to harass others for no reason. Even one of the guys in the group I that liked to hang out with was sort of a bully. It was as if I had some "KICK ME" sign taped to my back, or something. Halfway through the final block, I seemed to be having difficulty with my vision. The building started to become blurry. What was going on? Was it happening again?

The gem in my pocket began to shake. I looked down and there was the familiar glow in my right jeans pocket. As I caught sight of the faint light, I heard a voice calling my name.

The sickening spinning began to start and darkness set in. Where was I going now? What was next? Before I knew it, things were slowing down and my vision was beginning to clear up. When I could see again, I looked around and immediately recognized where I was. The starry ceiling and giant dragons every-where were dead giveaways that I was in Thiek's house.

"Knock, knock! Rise and shine! Lorenz, are you awake? It's Thiek!" Thiek was calling me merrily through my closed bedroom door. "Breakfast is done. Come and eat when you are ready!"

"Okay! Thanks, Thiek!" I replied to let him know I was up. I heard footsteps tap away down the hall.

I got up out of bed, got dressed, put my bag over my shoulders and headed out the door. I remembered the way to the kitchen and quickly worked my way there. Even though I had just eaten breakfast in the real world, my body here in this world was starving after sleeping all night, so I looked forward to Thiek's meal eagerly. I briefly wondered what he would make for me.

I saw Thiek in the kitchen, putting some pans away. "Good morning! I hope you enjoyed your room and slept well."

"I did. It's really nice. I had an interesting dream last night too," I mused.

"Oh! Those dreams can be very vivid!" cried Thiek.

"How do you know?" I asked as I sat down at the table.

"I've had a few of my own, of course." He was dressed in a new robe today. This time it was made of a silky grey light fabric with emerald hems. He walked over to me, carrying a plate of sliced fruit, cheese and buttered toasted, covered in chopped nuts.

"What do you mean by that?"

"Let's eat while we talk," replied Thiek. He started digging into his own plate. "Your dreams are training grounds for you to practice your skills. Especially when they are dreams that you've had before, you can react differently the second time and learn from the cause and effect of your mistakes. Tell me about your dream." said Thiek.

"Well, I don't remember too much about them, but I keep going back or for-ward in time." It was true. I knew that it had been a strange dream of significance, but I could hardly remember a thing about it.

"Hmmm…" Thiek rubbed his chin. "And what happens?" he asked.

"I go to places I've been to before, but things change usually when I'm faced with the same decisions I've had to deal with in past dreams."

"Do you make the same decisions over and over again?"

"No, I try other things. The outcome is different also." With his line of dream questioning, I almost felt like he were a therapist or fortune teller.

"Is that a good thing, changing your decisions?" asked Thiek.

"Yeah, I guess…" I trailed off, unsure. It was just a dream, I thought. Was this interrogation that important?

"Do you ever think the outcome might be very different, maybe even for the worse? If we change too many things in the past, the future becomes vastly differ-ent and you may lose what you've gained in the present."

"I think I understand…" I sounded a little dejected. "I just have a lot of bad dreams. I'd like to remind those in my past, who hurt me, what they put me through." I rubbed my face with the palm of my hand agitatedly. I thought of the painful memories I had with Bernard, Georgia, or my numerous schoolyard tormenters.

"How do you know they would understand? Do you believe that they would change?" asked Thiek.

"I don't know if they could understand how I felt or ever change, but it would make me feel better," I replied to him honestly.

"That is understandable." He had finished his meal, so he took his plate and my empty plate away to a sink and returned with a contemplative look. "You will face many difficult things and the people you meet will not always be easy to work with. That is why it is so important to make decisions where you think about both the outcomes of the immediate and long term futures."

I nodded and told him that I understood.

"With that said, your first task is about to take place. There is an ingredient that you must get for an important spell that you must learn," said Thiek. "The only place that it grows is in the small forest nearby. I will give you a map showing you how to get to it."

"What am I looking for?"

"Open up your spell book to the page with the basic healing spell. This spell and its variants will allow you to heal yourself, or even others, from mild injuries such as cuts, burns and bruises."

I did as he asked and took the tome out of my backpack. After turning the heavy leather cover and scanning each page, I found the healing spell just a few pages into the book. It did sound like a very useful beginning spell for me to learn. I liked knowing that I would be able to treat myself in case of an emergency.

"Once you have the ingredient, return back here and I'll help you prepare it for your spell. Can you read to me what the spell requires?"

I read the ingredients listing of the healing spell. It told me that I would need four young bwasan leaves. I relayed that information to Thiek, letting him know that I had found the answer.

"That's right. These leaves are found in the forest fifteen miles south of here. Once you've acquired them, you need to follow the directions in your spell book to make the potion. Do you understand everything thus far?"

"Yes," I answered him. "Am I going alone?"

"Yes, you are going alone. It is not too far and it will be a good learning experience for you. Remember all that you've learned so far about decisions you must make and whom you come into contact with. Trust your instincts in the face of danger."

By now, I felt warmed up and ready to go. I was excited about finally getting the chance to learn some cigam spells.

Thiek turned and went to a drawer under a counter nearby and grabbed what looked like a brown piece of parchment paper.

"Here is your map. Follow the map carefully and you won't get lost. Just re-member to think 'home' while holding the map in your right hand and it will show you how to get back here if you get lost. Be careful out there. Many things lurk in those woods."

"Got it." I hurried and got my backpack, adjusted my gear and was heading out the door. "I'm ready. I'll see you later then, Thiek. Bye! I'll be back before you know it!"

"See you soon," said Thiek with a small smile.

I closed the door behind me. Next thing I knew, I was on the path headed towards the main road. I checked the little map that Thiek gave me. There were the markings of mountains, cities, forests and other things of the local region. A little "X" scrawled on the forest in the map stood out to me and even jiggled a little on the paper, as if to grab my attention. It must be the place that Thiek was talking about. I put the map back into my pocket and kept walking.

I eventually walked my way up a small hill and once on the peak, I look back towards Thiek's house. I could see him, tiny in the distance, watching me from his front steps. I waved to him one final time and continued on my task.

The path going south took me into a wooded area. As I traveled the road, the woods became thicker and denser. I kept my guard up and alertly watched and listened to everything that I passed by. Little birds and woodland critters skittered and chattered all over the place. Before long, despite the bright morning sunlight, the path had become very dim and dappled through the heavy foliage of the forest canopy.

After about a half an hour traveling quietly this way, I heard the sounds of gruff voices talking on the path ahead of me. I stopped briefly to listen. I grabbed my sword from my backpack and hid myself behind one of the big trees off the main path, afraid that they might be wandering bandits.

The voices became louder and clearer as they approached closer. As they began to pass the tree I was hiding behind, I noticed that the sounds were coming from two very short people. They were only about three feet tall and stocky in build. Despite their small size, it was clear that these were adult men.

They were both muscular, rugged, clad in armor and carried deadly-looking weapons. The slightly taller one held an axe. The other had a bow and quiver on his back, full of serrated-tipped arrows. As they passed my tree, they spoke to each other in loud tones in a language that I couldn't understand.

After a moment, I realized that these creatures were dwarves. Suddenly, the taller one stopped in his tracks and turned towards me....

CHAPTER TWELVE

My blood froze in my veins. Did he notice me? But he wasn't quite looking in my direction. He turned towards me, but then looked upwards. I heard a noise coming from nearby me, up above. The tree branches were rustling very shakily as if something big were crawling around in the canopy. What in the world was up there?

While staying hidden, I looked up into the trees, but saw nothing but shivering leaves. Meanwhile, the taller dwarf said something and then they both took out their weapons. What was going on? I heard the trees rustle again and the sound was even closer now. I caught a brief glimpse of something in the trees. Whatever it was, it was very big.

It was a creature bigger than me. I had never seen anything like it before! It had curved horns on its large square head, an angular face with big slanted eyes, a pointy nose, and huge fangs protruded from its mouth. It grabbed the tree branches with its strong arms, hanging on with long fingers and claws. It also had fat legs and large wings. It was jumping from tree to tree with its thick, muscular legs and gripping the branches tightly with his hands each time it landed, like some kind of giant demon monkey. And now it was in the tree next to me.

The shorter dwarf aimed his bow with great skill and precision. He fired an arrow up into the tree with an audible twang of the bowstring. I heard a loud shriek along with the thud of the arrowhead hitting. Whatever that animal was, it had been creeping up on me, and the dwarf hit it.

The trees rustled again, raining down green leaves and little twigs. Presumably drawn by the sound of the wounded animal's pained shrieking, suddenly on the path south of the dwarves appeared another large horned creature. Then another one appeared to the north of them, surrounding them on the road. These guys looked like they were in trouble!

Then there was more rustling in the branches right above me. I looked up and there was another one looking down at me, snarling with big drops of saliva dripping from its open, toothy mouth. They were actively hostile now that one of their friends had been shot. It was coming right for me!

I couldn't fight this thing in this forest, tripping over roots and shrubs everywhere. I decided that I better go out into the open if I was going to get any sort of chance to defend myself. I ran out into the path that the other men were on and threw down my backpack for greater maneuverability. I would be much more mobile for battle without that heavy load on my back.

I was standing behind the monster facing the smaller dwarf. The creature didn't even know that I was behind it, so I decided I'd help out the dwarf by stabbing the creature from behind.

With my sword, I aimed for the creature's back. The blade hit square and true, tearing a wing and the creature let out a piercing shriek. It spun around and was attacking me now. To add to my problem, the one that had been tailing me from the tree had just reached us on the path as well.

They both bared their fangs at me, snarling and growling as slobber trickled from their jaws. I stepped backwards while holding my sword tightly and pointing it as menacingly at them as I could. I was terrified. I had never faced anything like this before. I glanced at the other men, hoping they would be able to help me, but it looked like the dwarves were each engaged in their own battles with other creatures that had shown up.

The monster with the torn wing took a swipe at me with its claws, and then attempted to bite me. It missed on each of its attempts. Each time it attacked, I took a step back or to the left or right. After its last attempt to chomp at me, which left its head and neck vulnerable and outstretched, I aimed my sword and tried to slash at it.

My sword was far less effective on this thick-skinned beast than it had been on Jbug and his company. The monster screamed as the blade cut its flesh superficially and it lunged at me, missing again. I dodged and kept trying to counterattack. Again, my attempt was to no avail. After several exchanges like this, it was clearly becoming frustrated.

It reared its head ferociously and sliced at me once more as I stepped to the left and swung my sword.

"Agh!" I cried out as I doubled over in pain. The monster had left bleeding gashes on my chest and arm. They were not serious wounds though, thanks to my armor. My own blade had hit the creature's right shoulder, opening the skin to the shoulder bone. It was rearing its head and hissing.

While the creature expressed its anger, I looked and saw the dwarves making progress in their own fights. I didn't get to watch them long though, because the beast came at me in a wild rage, leaving another tear in my armor with its long nails.

My clothing was becoming a bunch of wretched rags and would soon be of little protection to me. I suddenly remembered the armor in my backpack. I quickly reached in to grab my shield, but the creature charging at me suddenly stumbled forward, as one of its companions had crashed into it from behind, with arrows in his throat. I took this opportunity to try to make my final blow.

Aiming for the heart, my sword pierced its skin and with me throwing all of my body weight into it, the blade went through. The creature twitched and jerked violently as it died. The monster that the dwarven archer had brought down was also in its death spasms. Finally, everything was quiet now that the fighting was over, as the other beasts had run away after seeing their friends fall to us.

The larger dwarf, covered in blood, some of which was his own, laid his axe down and knelt by one of the dead beasts. He felt the creature's neck and face, as if looking for its pulse or breath. Then the larger dwarf's steely eyes caught mine. He stopped and then spoke something to the other dwarf. They both began to slowly walk towards me.

I backed up a step, hanging onto my sword, ready to defend myself. They were probably upset that I had obviously been hiding and watching them behind the trees. I wondered if I should try to say something to them. Their eyes turned to the creature I had killed for a moment and then flitted back to me.

Then the shorter dwarf's look turned to happy surprise and he smiled. "If ya hadn'ta shown up-ah, we mighta been in some-ah trouble!"

He apparently could speak English, but his accent was very thick and a little hard to understand. He also paused to think about his words often. I had to really concentrate to pick out what he was saying.

"My name is Unni an'-ah this is-ah here's, my brother, Okin-ah. We are-ah from the village o' Josieah in-ah the region o' TiVir."

"I am Lorenz from NotingShaw." I introduced myself, thinking about extending my hand for a shake, but then changed my mind when I realized how dirty and bloody it was. I rubbed my grimy hand on my clothes sheepishly. It was just as well. Their hands weren't any cleaner than mine after that intense battle.

"Because-ah ya helped us-ah, we're in-ah debt ta ya."

"The feeling is mutual," I told him. "Where were you going?"

"We were-ah goin' tah the nearest town-ah south."

This sounded like it might be convenient for us to work out a cooperative deal. "I'm headed south too! Would you like to join me? We could travel all together."

"What's in it-ah for us?"

"Things you find while traveling, you keep!" I told them cheerfully. It sounded like a decent deal to me.

The taller dwarf looked contemplative. Okin said something to his brother Unni. He nodded and said okay.

After agreeing, they started checking the dead monsters and Okin had found a little gold key on one of them. We figured that the key unlocked something of great worth.

"For-ah helpin' us out, I will-ah share-ah what is foun' with this-ah key if ya help us fin' what it unlocks."

I agreed, but I told them I had to collect some leaves from this forest first for my teacher, a ways further down the path. The brothers looked at each other and said something that I didn't understand, and then agreed.

We three traveled south. As we followed a long bend in the road, we found that the road began to branch off into a small pathway that led up into the trees. We stopped for a minute to see if we could see further up this curious new path, but we could see nothing because the thick trees blocked our view. We decided to check it out.

Unni ran ahead excitedly and then plodded up the small path casually looking around. The path didn't go very far into the woods and dead ended at a house. He called to us to hurry over to him.

"There's a house up-ah there."

"What does it look like?" I asked him as Okin and I were catching up.

"I-ah can't-ah see it-ah tha' well. Ya wan' me tah go closer?"

Okin and I agreed to let him scout out the abandoned-looking house on his own first. He ran surprisingly fast for such a short guy. The dwarves had an astounding amount of strength and energy for their size.

He went about the property and called out to us any details he noticed. The house was really old and made of huge bricks of quarried stone. There were also three white columns arranged in a big triangle in front of the house. They were made of marbled stone and decorated with a curly floral motif at each end. The columns were all topped with huge granite spheres and it looked like something used to sit on top of these spheres.

After he finished his recon description, Okin and I decided to follow after Unni and got a look for ourselves. As we traveled up the weathered walkway to the house, I heard a shuffling noise coming from behind me. I stopped and turned around to see if there was anything following us, but saw nothing behind us. The dwarves had continued looking around without me. When I finally reached the brothers, I heard the sound again coming from my left. I decided to mention this to them.

"Did you guys hear that noise?"

"What-ah noise?" replied Unni, cupping his hand to his ear to listen. He got a serious look in his eye and grabbed his brother by the shoulder and signaled to him to listen too. They both listened for the sound together.

Unni silently pulled out his bow and an arrow and Okin took his axe from his belt. Trusting their experience, I followed their suit by pulling out my own sword in turn.

We spread out to give each other room to run or fight, and scanned our surroundings with great alertness, listening intently. From the darkness of the forest trees, out came a large creature.

It had a lot of legs. Countless pearly eyes glittered on top of its furry head and oozing fangs protruded from its mouth. The body was covered in marble-white hairs, from head to toe. It looked kind of like a spider, except it was the size of a buffalo. It could scarcely even maneuver between the trees because of its large size.

It came towards us, taking advantage of the open space of the pathway and front lot. As the creature advanced, its iridescent fur shone like opal in the sunlight.

I moved away from the spider. I backed down the path, shuffling backwards, careful not to trip over anything on the ground. Meanwhile, Unni backed up towards the edge of the other side of the path, into the tree line. Okin moved backwards up the path in an opposite direction. We were triangulating our positions to surround the monster in case it decided to aggress further.

As I backed away from it, the creature attempted to swipe at me with one of its clawed legs. It missed. The ugly monstrosity continued to follow me with its clawed front legs raised aggressively. Clearly, it wasn't going to back down. Again, it tried to hit me and missed. It was my turn now.

Getting the hang of how this creature moved and attacked, I swung my sword at the leg that had just grazed the air by me. My sword struck the leg and chipped the appendage's hard exoskeleton. Clear yellowish blood oozed from the wound. The spider-like beast let out a buzzing, shrieking sound of pain, vibrating the very air around me, making my ears ring.

Recognizing this chance to strike, Okin charged forward and made a daring leap, bringing his axe down on another leg in range. It was a good, hard blow, completely severing the lower segments of the limb. At the same time, Unni also struck the creature in a different leg with a well-aimed arrow.

The unspoken plan was working. The creature's balance was now compromised and it staggered. As the huge spider monster stumbled over itself, blood kept spewing from the legs all around. Seeing that this was our opportunity to kill the creature, all three of us attacked it—each of us striking the creature, with Unni dealing the final blow.

As the monster fell onto its back in death, its long, spindly legs began to curl up just like a dead spider's. It gave me the shivers looking at the thing. We worried that, like with the horned beasts from before, there might be more of these coming, so I suggested that we go to hide in the house up the path. The dwarves agreed. It could make a safe place for us to rest and catch our breath.

We walked up to the house cautiously, with each of us monitoring a different side. It sure helped having companions. It made things much safer than traveling alone. Luckily, we reached the top of the house without encountering any other problems.

It was an unusual two story mansion. The huge house was very square, but it had windows that were triangle in shape. Two tall isosceles triangle windows flanked each side of the front door. The massive entrance was made of rusted iron and was almost three times my height. There was a front courtyard before us, made of beautiful bricks inlaid in the ground, making a colorful mosaic. This was where the hourglass-shaped columns stood.

As we approached the white pillars, Unni stopped me by gently grabbing my arm. He shook his head and picked up two loose rocks from the ground and threw the first into the center of the three pillars and then the second one far past them. For a second, I wondered what he was doing, but then I realized that he was checking for booby traps. That was a good idea. I was usually more careful than this, but had let my guard down since I felt safer in the group.

I copied him and threw an even bigger rock. It clacked on the ground and rolled, hitting the base of one of the columns and stopping. None of our attempts had set off any traps, so we continued walking.

By now, we had reached the foot of the stone steps to the large house. The enormous doorway loomed down at us.

"What-ah do ya think is inside?" asked Unni.

Okin shook his head and I just shrugged.

"What does that mean?" asked Okin, puzzled about my shoulder shrugging.

"Oh, it just means that I don't know either."

Okin sighed jokingly. "Humans..."

"Anyways, maybe there's something important inside the house," I said. "I wonder if that monster was guarding this place."

"What-ah makes ya say that?" he asked.

"Well, there's nothing on the top of the pillars anymore. Also, the pillars are the same colors as the monster we killed." It was true that both the pillars and the monster were a brilliant white.

The taller brother gestured towards the door before us. "Who's-ah goin' in first?" Before either of us could even respond, Okin started towards the steps.

Unni stopped him to remind him to check for traps first, so Okin began prodding each step with his axe before putting his foot down on them.

There didn't seem to be anything unusual on the stairs or on the porch. Finally, we just had to check the door. We saw that there were numerous gashes and scratches in the door all around the triangular bronze knob, as if someone or something had been trying to break in. Nothing strange was on the door or knob itself, though. "It seems safe to touch," I said. "What about the lock?"

"I don' see a lock." said Unni, scrutinizing the doorway.

"Then the door must be open?" I asked them. "Let's check it out!" I started to grab the knob. I suddenly remembered how the voice had told me that I should pay attention to my surroundings and how Thiek had told me to be careful. As my right hand surrounded the knob, it suddenly felt very cold. It felt as if it had been in a freezer! Alarmed, I yanked my hand away from the knob, fearing it was some kind of trap and might be frozen.

I released the knob without difficulty and breathed a sigh of relief. I put my hand back on the knob slowly and turned the knob clockwise. As the knob turned, I could feel my heart beat louder. After I felt it click, I backed away, letting the door slowly swing open with a creak.

I peeked into the doorway. I could hardly see anything besides the darkness inside and then the door slammed itself shut without any warning.

Surprised by the door moving on its own like that, we all looked around to see if we saw anything. We looked left, right, at the door, on the walls, the columns, and then turned our eyes to the spherical stones on top of the columns.

They now had something perched on top of each of them. What were they? Where did they come from? They looked like stony gargoyles, but whatever they were, there were three of them.

They were each hunched over with their backs to us. Okin raised his axe in preparation of attack. Unni immediately told him in a soft voice to stand down and try not to provoke the trio of guardians.

"Don't-ah bother them. You might-ah make-ah them come alive."

Okin nodded.

"Yeah, let's not initiate a fight. Let's try and get into this house if we can," I stressed. "Watch the creatures on top of the columns. Watch my back!" I told Okin and Unni. I went to the door and tried to turn the knob, but it wouldn't budge. I tried harder, but no matter how I pulled or pushed, the door would no longer open. I was now feeling frustrated and thinking about breaking the door in, when my gut feeling told me to just move on.

I stopped and suggested to them, "Let's leave this place. The door won't open for us right now. Let's head for the main path and get my leaves."

The dwarves looked unenthusiastic about my proposal. "But-ah what about the house and-ah the key?" asked Unni.

"We can come back to this house later."

"Somebody might-ah break in and-ah take-ah what's inside before us!" retorted Okin.

I tried to reason with them carefully, not wanting to make them angry. "We don't know what's inside the house yet. Plus, it's starting to get dark. Don't you think we should go before nighttime? At night, who knows what we may face. These new creatures may or may not attack us also."

"Maybe you're-ah right." Unni nodded in agreement.

Okin shrugged, using his newly learned human expression. He began to walk off, back the way we had come.

"Wait!" I said. "We have to leave carefully. Remember, we don't know if those things on top of the columns are alive or aggressive."

"Let's-ah see." said Okin. He bent down with the intention to pick up a rock to throw.

I quickly grabbed him on the shoulder and shook my head from side to side. "Uh-uh, not a good idea!"

Unni looked at Okin saying, "Are-ah ya crazy!? Those-ah thin's might attack us!"

"Okay, okay." Okin replied.

"We need to get out of here." I said. "Okin, you take the back, Unni, you get the middle and I'll take the front. Let's try and ease our way out of here."

So we started slowly leaving the house. I headed away from the house, feeling relieved knowing that I had Unni and Okin watching my back. We went in a straight line, single file. When we walked past the columns, we looked upwards at the pillars to see if the creatures had moved. They hadn't budged an inch, so we kept on moving, hoping they wouldn't cause us any trouble.

When we finally got back to the main road, I asked them, "Where should we set up camp? What do you think if we set up camp on the other side of the road there?"

"What's-ah wrong-a with-ah this-ah side of-ah the road?' asked Okin, feeling lazy and wanting to pitch camp right there.

Ever the thoughtful one, Unni replied to him, "Those-ah creatures on-ah the columns-ah might attack us for-ah one. We also killed-ah tha' spidah no' far-ah from-ah here too, remembah?"

"Ya, I forgot abou' that," said Okin, laughing a little.

With that, we cut across and went down the road to put some distance between us and the mysterious house. We made sure that no one and nothing was following us. There had been too many close encounters today. Okin even went ahead of us and into the trees and bushes to see if he saw anything. Nothing dangerous was around.

We kept going, looking for a nice little clearing where we could set up camp safely. We soon came upon an inviting spot. All three of us noticed it and decided upon it at the same time. It was a large patch of soft meadow grass shaded by overhanging fruiting tree branches, hidden just behind some scrubby shrubs. There was fallen timber nearby that we could use for firewood and some logs we could prop up for seating. The suns were now approaching the horizon, casting everything in a dim orange glow. The moon had taken its place in the sky, now shining bright and clear.

We heard various sounds such as leaves rustling in the wind, branches crackling, and animals skittering around. There were animal sounds that I didn't recognize, like different hoots, snorts, croaks and chirps. Though I didn't know what was making the noises, I wasn't afraid. I was curious about what sorts of animals they were and what they might look like. In my short time in this world, I had seen so many new things and heard so many sounds I had never heard before.

One sound in particular sounded like a short shrieking scream. Maybe it was some kind of nocturnal bird. When we first heard the piercing shriek, we all immediately took out our weapons. When we realized that it was just a distant bird call however, we laughed it off, feeling relieved and amused at our tenseness.

Before we could set up camp, we had to make sure that the surrounding area was completely safe. Okin volunteered to scout out the forest around our campsite, checking the trees for hidden beasts.

He disappeared through the darkness and trees. Night was setting in quickly now. The moonlight shone through the branches and foliage, dappling everything beneath them in pale white light. I could see Okin's silvery silhouette darting about between tree trunks and shrubs. Unni and I kept watch in all directions, down the path and the wilderness around us. Nothing was going to catch us off guard this time.

A few minutes later, Okin came shuffling through the trees and bushes with a smile on his face. "Looks-ah good ta me!"

"Boy, that was fast! Great work, Okin!" I congratulated him and slapped him jovially on the back.

We all followed Okin back through the huge trees towards the clearing. The tree trunks around the clearing had green mossy plant growth on them, as it was damp and dewy in the shade. Patches of round mushrooms and fairy rings decorated the grassy ground. Tufts of flowering weeds and herbs dotted the little meadow.

We checked the area for man-made dangers as well as for natural ones. There didn't appear to be any booby traps or signs of recent human life anywhere here. While it looked like people had camped here before long ago, evident from the sawn off branches and logs we found, no one was here now and no one had been staying here for a long time. This nice camping spot was all ours at the moment.

Okin started to set up a campfire, digging out a small pit in the ground with his axe and his hands. With the sunlight gone, we would need the warmth. Most of all, we needed the light to do any work by, like setting up camp. With some effort, he used tinder and flint stone he had in his pockets to start some glowing red embers. He blew on them gently, coaxing them to grow into little flickers of flame until they had grown large and strong enough to begin to consume the small dry branches he began to feed them.

Unni set up a simple oil lantern for some light for himself and gave me a small lantern to use too. It was a beautiful polished stone lamp with a little hole for a burning wick and a hole in the center for refilling it with more oil. I thanked him for the gift and lit it up with the help of the small fire that Okin had just started. The warm yellow glow of the firelight, the smell of the smoke and burning wood, and the quiet crackling of the firewood was mesmerizing and allowed me to finally relax my weary body and mind.

I soon had to shake out of my trance because we had to start setting up camp. I had never really set up camp before, so I watched Okin take out his tenting materials from a big leather purse he carried and saw how he set it up. Unni did the same with his own tent. They set up a basic framework first of sticks or rods, draped the tent material over it, and fastened everything down with little tethering ropes.

"Wow, you guys are quick!" I complimented them about their swift tent skills.

"We're-ah use' to it," replied Okin, grinning from the praise.

I felt a little left out because I had never got a tent and wondered what I should do. I turned my lantern towards my backpack and search around in it for something I could use as a makeshift tent, to cover myself up for the night. Nothing at first was usable, but then I felt something like a thin, sheer cloth all folded up.

I grabbed the item and pulled it out. "I don't remember having this in my bag?" I mused aloud.

It was a big drawstring pouch of dark color, a deep purple. It was also a little shiny, like satin or silk, with golden string. With this kind of gaudy color scheme, I knew it had to be from Thiek. He must have slipped this into my bag when I was asleep or eating breakfast earlier today. I smiled and thanked him silently. I wasn't absolutely sure what was inside yet, but I had a hunch as to what it was, and it would be useful.

I pulled open the shiny purple bag and reached inside. I pulled out a big folded up hide. It was a leathery brown skin treated to be water resistant and so it was also soft and easy to work with. Once I had taken it out, I knew my hunch was correct. Thiek had thoughtfully packed me a tent to sleep under.

I started to put my tent together. After watching Okin and Unni pitch their tents, I had most of the idea how to do it. They also were there to help me whenever I needed an extra hand in setting the frame or tying something down taut. Without realizing it, I had the tent built in no time. I was amazed at how quickly I was able to do it on my first try. Done! Tent was set up and I was ready for bed.

Unni and Okin were going around the campsite gathering dried up leaves, twigs and branches to keep nearby to stock the fire.

"What do we do now?" I asked them. "Someone has to be up to feed the fire and make sure nothing sneaks up on us in the night."

Unni grunted in approval and nodded. "We haff to split up-ah the night into three watches."

We discussed who would take what shift. Each shift would be approximately three hours long. Okin was used to doing the first shift, so he got to be the first watch. Unni would be second, which worked out because I had no idea how I would know that three hours had passed without a clock. I would have the final watch after getting about six hours of sleep and then we'd pack up and go with the rising sun.

I went into my shiny purple tent to rest and Unni went into his. Okin stayed out in the middle of the clearing next to the fire. As I went in, I saw him take out a small dagger and start whittling a piece of wood. I went in and lay down on the leather hide flooring. The ground was hard and bumpy through the hide, and without fluffy blankets and pillows, it was pretty uncomfortable and chilly. But I was so tired from all the walking and fighting today that as soon as my head hit the ground, I sensed myself falling into a deep sleep. All the tension in my muscles melted away as I relaxed and drifted off.

CHAPTER THIRTEEN

When I awoke, I was surprised to find my vision hazy. I rubbed my eyes, trying to clear them. I then noticed a number of houses on both sides of the street. Wait a minute, what street? I wasn't in the forest campsite anymore with Okin and Unni! I was now standing in the middle of a sidewalk. I felt a little frustrated that my situation in the forest with the dwarves was being interrupted. I wondered what they were doing now and if we were all okay. This jumping between worlds was always happening at awkward times.

The houses around me all had cement steps leading up to their front door-step. They were brick with square windows all around with chimneys on top. It was beginning to feel familiar to me. I was approaching a large red brick complex of buildings. They had decorative columns lining the outdoor walkways between them. Stadium lights, flag poles, and electronic bulletin boards towered over them. I recognized what this was. It was my new school. It was my first day in the 7th grade now. I was finally in middle school.

As I continued to walk, I began to remember where I was, what day it was and where I was going. My family and I had recently moved to this area from the other side of town. This area was much nicer. There was far less crime, the streets were clean, and the people were friendlier. Here, people watered and mowed their lawns, rather than have miniature wastelands of garbage-strewn weeds accenting their houses. No one even had to lock their mailboxes here. Best of all was my new living situation at home.

We now lived in a two story house with three bedrooms. It was a real house of our own, not some little apartment or townhouse. We had a front porch with a swinging bench to lounge on and a decently sized backyard with a garden to play in. Darius and I had even played catch together the other day. We had a living room, dining room, and even a basement! Man, this was exciting! While walking the rest of the way to school, these thoughts ran happily through my mind.

My first day at school would be straightforward. This morning, I had eaten breakfast at home, so I was still stuffed and happy, full of pancakes and sausage. I just came into the auditorium and registered with my mom after waiting in a long line full of other students and their parents. We got to meet the vice principal and other faculty members. Everyone was so nice; they all smiled and shook hands and spoke warmly to each other. This seemed like a cool school. I looked forward to when Darius would be old enough to attend with me.

The numerous pairs of double sided doors were open for people to walk in for orientation. The school's walls were painted green and blue, which were our school colors. Glass cabinets lined the walls of some of the hallways. They were filled with all sorts of shining medals, ribbons and trophies.

I didn't get the chance to stop and read them, but from the photographs displayed alongside them, I could see that they were for various physical and academic competitions. Students in jerseys, girls posed in cheerleader dresses, and mock trial students in business casual all smiled back at me as I passed them. I wondered how all these kids were doing now—actually, some of these "kids" were my mom's age or older by now, judging from the dates. As I admired the pictures, one photo in particular caught my eye.

A marching band full of beaming students in sharp white uniforms, proudly holding their instruments, stood in a huge green football field. I found the orderly formations, glam and sound of the drums and brass in a marching band very invigorating. I told my mother excitedly, "I want to be in the band too! I'll find out how to sign up for the band soon."

After orientation and registration were over, my mom went home and I got to finish the rest of my day at school, seeing my new classes and teachers, and getting a feel for the new campus.

As I walked up the stairs, I walked alongside many students dressed in warm clothes because of the cool autumn weather. Scarves, coats and boots were common. I was in earmuffs and a windbreaker myself. Most students also carried books and tablets as they headed to their classes. Everyone's clothes and accessories were bright and shiny and new, just recently bought by excited parents for their kids for the new school year. I walked up the staircase on the right, wondering if any of the people next to me were in my class.

I reached the next floor. I checked the numbers on the brown-painted doors of the hallway. They each had a rectangular plastic window to see into the classroom and the classroom number would be displayed in bold white numbers on a little placard underneath.

"Room 217, huh?" I thought aloud to myself while searching and moving my way through the crowd. I needed to get to room 320. It would be the classroom where I would start my school days. I needed to wind my way up another flight of stairs. I turned and went up the stairway, almost bumping into another student. I held onto the wide metal banister for support.

After reaching the third floor, I was at the top. There were no more steps to go higher, though there was a faculty-only door that seemed to lead up to the rooftop for maintenance work. After looking at the number of the room closest to me, I found that I was now at 317. I needed to turn left or right at this intersection, so I went to the right, hoping that the numbers on the doors would increase. The room number was 319, so I was on the right track. My room would be next.

So there I was, at room 320. Boy, I was nervous now! It was my first day in middle school and I didn't know anyone here yet. I took a deep breath and reached for the round knob and began to turn it. I looked up briefly to see inside the plastic window and saw the teacher sitting at the desk.

The teacher was a woman with long, wavy, black hair down to her shoulders who wore a long sepia-toned dress. There were numerous books on her desk and stacks of papers too. No doubt, she would be passing those out to the class any minute now. "Better not be late," I told myself. I stepped inside the room.

There were about thirty metal student desks arranged in rows. They had a compartment for storing books in, under the writing surface which was topped with a wood veneer. Most of the desks on the far side of the room were already taken by other students, both boys and girls. I looked for an open desk to sit down. I was even more nervous now.

As looked for the open desk, I looked at each student briefly, seeing what type of reaction I would get and wondering what kind of personalities they had. I would probably become friends with some of these kids soon. Many were looking down shyly or arranging their school supplies on their desk, some were talking, and a few sleepyheads were just laying their heads down. Others were looking at the teacher. She had not started the class yet.

There was an empty desk in the front corner that I decided to take. I sat my school backpack down, which was still light because I didn't have any textbooks yet. A few minutes later, I had gotten out my papers, binder and pencil, all ready for class. I had a plain black binder with several hole-punched folders to arrange my notes and homework. I also had brought with me in my backpack some ballpoint pens and several mechanical pencils with 0.7 mm #2 lead, perfect for using on any tests. Despite my preparedness, I was so nervous that I knew I needed to try and calm down. Mostly, I was worried about making friends and about being bullied. I really wanted to be able to enjoy going to school for once.

The bell rang, indicating that it was time for class. After a few moments of looking around to wait for the students to settle down, the teacher got up and started. She wrote something on the green chalkboard at the front of the classroom. As she wrote, I looked around the classroom briefly, noticing I could see numerous posters, pictures and other things on the walls. She explained that this would be our homeroom, which was where we would take attendance, say the pledge of allegiance, and do other miscellaneous administrative things like buying school lunch tickets. She also told us what the goals and expectations of her class were, as our homeroom doubled as a history class.

After a few minutes more of talking, she handed out some books. They were thick and heavy hardcover textbooks, so she had to go back a few times to her desk to bring them to the students. The book had an image with ancient statues and soldiers on the cover. It was a history book. She told us that we needed to bring our books every day or else there would be some kind of consequence.

The rest of the morning went fine. Most of my classes occurred on the third floor. Aside from history, I also had English, pre-algebra, and biology. Personally, my favorite class was my last period class—an elective that I chose—woodshop.

Woodshop was on the first floor and the large room was filled with big machines and numerous piles of lumber. Examples of carved and sawn goods like furniture and figurines were displayed on some high shelves. The place smelled of motor oil and sawdust, which was surprisingly more pleasant than I had originally imagined. Instead of desks, there were large rectangular counters that were connected to the floor. Tall metal stools stood by the counters for people to work on. There were all sorts of special drills and saws specialized in cutting wood. They seemed dangerous if used carelessly, but the teacher would show us how to work with the tools appropriately to do all sorts of fun and creative projects.

The woodshop teacher was an older gray haired man just a smidge over six feet tall, in a checkered red and blue shirt and corduroys. He had calloused hands and thick strong arms from decades of working with tools and huge pieces of timber.

We didn't have a book for this class, but he gave us some papers to read and take home to sign before we were allowed to work with any of the tools. I couldn't wait to get home to get my mom to sign it. It reminded me of the time I had to get her signature for working in the school parade. Though my part of my split consciousness hadn't been in my body at the time of the parade, I was glad to still have memories of the fun event.

The bell rang and it was time to return to homeroom. As I had done earlier that morning, I went past the office and up two flights of stairs. Unlike my last school, we had to come back to our homeroom briefly before the end of the school day to take attendance again and get any announcements or fliers pertinent to our classes or the school in general.

I sat down and sat my chin down briefly on the top of the desk, feeling a little winded. I guess I was just getting tired from all the excitement of the first day, worrying and trying to take in so much. Everything was already packed away in my backpack in anticipation of the imminent bell.

Right after the bell, a female student got up and started to walk by. She was a tall, but heavy set African American with fairly light skin and a very unfriendly expression. Her short hair had obviously been curly before, but was permed and straightened. She was at least part Asian, as she had narrow almond-shaped eyes. Her narrowed eyes only made her look even angrier along with her sour countenance. She came down my row walking between the two rows of desks, shooting people ugly looks. Geez, obviously she wasn't having a good day and was trying her best to let everyone else know. I sighed and looked away from her.

She began to walk past me, but she was only halfway past my desk when I suddenly felt a pain on my head. My head immediately jerked back due to the force of the pull on my hair. She had just yanked my hair! Without even thinking, I jumped up, turned to face her and slapped her in the face.

There was a loud roar of amusement and surprise from the classroom after they noticed what just happened. The students stood up; the teacher stood up. They were all staring at us. This had never happened to me before. I wasn't even aware that my hand had connected. I felt dizzy and disoriented and scared. My gut told me to take a step back. I was only able to take a half a step backwards before I bumped into another desk and I felt something hit my chin. It hit me hard; it was the girl's fist. She was taller, wider and heavier than me and packed a lot force into that punch. The crowd around me roared and the teacher shouted something.

I felt myself fall backwards, crashing noisily into some desks, though I tried to get back up and defend myself. I felt pain and I could tell that I was on the ground, unable to move. My body hurt in many places, especially my face where she had hit me. My lip felt warm and wet; the skin had been split, smearing blood across my chin. I clenched my eyes shut. Everything was so noisy and my vision was blurred with bright stars. Then everything faded to black.

Next thing I knew, I was in a dark place and my face didn't hurt anymore. I touched my lip, which was intact, and felt around to try and find something to orient myself. The first thing I felt was supple leather drawn tight across wooden beams. I soon realized that I was back in Thiek's gaudy tent.

I grabbed hold of the opening flap to my tent and pulled it open slowly, peeking outside. Unni was sitting alone by the small campfire, warming his hands. After realizing that things were okay, I decided to get some shut eye, as I would need to get up soon to do my watch. First, I decided to go and ask him how much longer it was until my turn.

I got up, went outside the tent and headed towards Unni. Hearing my footsteps, he jumped up and aimed his bow and arrow at me without hesitation.

"It's me!!" I yelped, flinging my arms in front of my chest and face defensively.

He immediately lowered his bow and arrow. "Sorry, Lorenz-ah, lad. I wasn't-ah sure!"

"I just came out to ask you when do you want me to start my watch?" I lowered my hands after he recognized me, but my heart was still pounding in my chest.

"I still-ah have a coupla hours."

"All right, I'll relieve you in a couple hours then." I waved to him and then went back into my tent to rest some more. Within minutes I was back asleep, as my body here was still so tired from the journeying.

I was awakened by a slight noise. It sounded like someone scratching something coarse. "What is that?" I mumbled, rubbing my eyes. I rolled over to face the entrance of the tent and noticed a short figure whose shadow was looming over the entrance. I figured that it was Unni telling me it was time to do my watch. "I'm coming," I told him, so that he could stop scratching at my door. I immediately put on my gear and grabbed my sword.

I got up, walked out of the tent and headed towards the campfire that was burning. Unni was gathering his stuff as he headed back towards his tent.

"Good night, Unni."

"Good-ah night!" the dwarf replied sleepily.

I immediately found and picked up some broken branches that were sitting not too far from the fire. Unni had left a pile there for me. I picked up a couple of pieces and tossed them into the fire. The flames rose happily as they consumed the sticks. I watched the branches blacken and curl in the heat. The weather wasn't too cold, but it felt nice and toasty to have the fire built up a little higher.

I sat down and looked at the fire thinking about Thiek and the quest he had sent me on. I wondered how far away the bwasan leaves were from here. Was I taking too much time off from Thiek's task? I didn't know if I should go back to the abandoned-looking house even though it had originally been my intention to. It was really dangerous at that old house, the rewards within were unknown and it would take a lot of my time that I ought to have been spending following Thiek's and the Creator's missions. I didn't know how I could tell Unni and Okin about my current hesitation without upsetting them, though.

Suddenly I heard a sound that made me jump up and snap out of my thoughts. What I heard was the crackling of wood… but it wasn't coming from the fire.

I made sure that my things were safe and tried to make out whatever it was in the darkness. Whatever had made that noise, it wasn't going away. In fact, it was rapidly coming closer. I could hear the cracking and rustling of twigs and dried leaves.

"What is it? Is it an animal? Is it human?" I asked breathily to myself, trying to keep my spirits up and dispel my fears.

I tried to feel it out with my gut instincts, like Thiek and the Creator had suggested me to do before. What was it? I closed my eyes briefly and listened. Somehow, I got the feeling that it was nothing serious and nothing to be afraid of. I had a hard time believing my intuition this time. I thought I'd better check to make sure. I didn't want to wake up Okin or Unni in case it was a false alarm, so I just stepped out into the brush myself. After each step, I stopped to listen for sounds and look around in the darkness, however much that helped.

After a while, I heard nothing but the rustling of the wind with the leaves and the trees. "Maybe whatever was there is gone?" I looked back towards the camp. Everything looked like it was fine. I shrugged off my suspicions about wild beasts and decided to head back to the fire.

Once I had settled back down, I thought I'd pass the time looking at my spell book. Thiek had wanted me to study it, so this quiet night by the fire might be a good opportunity.

I grabbed my bag and pulled out the spell book. I flipped to the page most relevant to me at the moment, which was the page with the healing spell.

I read through the page quickly, picking out the important details. I had to break the leaves into pieces and put them into boiling water with a certain tree branch. After the leaves blanched in the hot water, the solution could be dripped onto a minor wound along with an incantation. I also read that this spell wouldn't work if the wound was more than a day old. More powerful spells must be used for those.

There were so many arbitrary little rules and incantations. This book, being so thick, was a lot to study, but it must have so many incredible spells to use. I was excited about learning more. As I continued to read in my spell book, I could hear the crackling of branches and leaves again in the shrubs near us. The wind was now still enough that I could easily hear what direction the noise was coming from. I immediately grabbed my sack, put my spell book away and picked up my sword, which was lying right next to me within easy reach. I stood up to face it.

The big question was: do I go it alone, not knowing what I'd face, or do I wake up the guys? If I woke them up, I'd have help. If I do it myself, unprepared and not knowing what's out there, I might get hurt or killed.

"This should be a no brainer. Of course I should go and wake them up. Why would I want to fight alone?" Then a thought came to me. I wanted to see how good I was on my own. It seemed like a pretty reckless idea though. It certainly wasn't a good enough reason to fight whatever was out there alone.

As I debated with myself, whatever was out there was moving away from the fire because the sounds were getting softer and farther away. It seemed as if it wasn't going to come up to the campsite after all. My curiosity got the better of me and I decided that I could at least investigate it.

I put on my backpack and kept my sword in hand. I would check it out alone, just briefly. "What could be out there anyway? It's walking away. It can't be that big or dangerous!" I reasoned to myself with some forced bravado. If my gut could talk, it would be screaming at me not to do such a foolish thing, but I ignored that twisting pit in my stomach and pressed on.

Before heading out, I grabbed an unused torch which had been left on the ground by one of the dwarves, and stuck it into the fire to light it. I had a source of light now and I could also use it as a defensive weapon, like adventurers always did in the movies. I crept along as quietly as I could, towards the direction where the quiet shuffling sounds were coming from.

I lifted my torch, holding it out in front of me to light my way ahead. The fire cast a yellow glow upon everything and shadows danced along as I walked by. I could hardly even see the bright white moon through all the dense tree foliage. It was good I had brought a torch, as it would have been very dark without it.

The skittering sounds now were emanating from a thicket of brambly bushes in front of me. My heart began to beat faster and faster, with the realization that I was about to face something that might be very dangerous. I could just barely make out the broken up silhouette of something through the thick plant cover.

It was long. It was well over twelve feet long, actually, and it was very low to the ground. I might have thought that it was some kind of big snake, except that when it suddenly turned to face me, staring at me with big green eyes, there were long antennae sticking out of its head and waving at me.

The creature had noticed me and now was coming straight for me. Its long, thick body was sort of flattened and flanked on each side by countless sharp, spindly legs. Its tail end was also tipped with a pair of long feelers. Illuminated by my torchlight, the creature's eyes appeared to glow ominously and it gnashed its huge fangs hungrily. This was some kind of enormous centipede! If that was the case, those fangs were probably venomous!

Then, it let out an awful screech. I knew that venomous centipede or not, I needed to make the first strike. It reared up and prepared itself for attack. I knew this was it. I wasn't prepared for what was going on, but since I had recklessly gone so far away from camp, it was just me and the monster now.

I stepped back, trying to keep some distance from it, trying to figure out where to attack first. I knew that the head would be tough to hit because it was raised so high. I just couldn't let it hit me first…

I kept moving away from the head and closer to the tail. It seemed like a safe place to attack since there were no harmful appendages on the tail end. Within a few feet away, I attempted to strike the tail of the creature, but missed. It had drawn its tail away from me surprisingly fast.

As I recovered from my strike attempt, I saw it lunge for me through the corner of my eye. I dove out of the way and it thankfully missed, but I dropped my torch and it went out from the impact with ground. I couldn't see very well now, but I had to keep trying my best. I stumbled over some fallen logs, but recovered quickly enough to take another swing at its tail. This time, it connected. One of the feelers was sliced off.

The creature screamed in pain, thrashing its head. It immediately turned towards me to strike. With all of the angry force it could muster, it hurtled its fanged face towards me, missing, and getting a face full of leaves and dirt. I had just barely jumped out the way in time and landed hard on some rocks and tree roots, wincing and crying out in pain.

The centipede monster, seeing that I was on the ground, once again reared itself up menacingly. It prepared to make the killing strike. It then howled again, shuddered violently and then its head fell to the ground lifeless. I stopped immediately, not knowing what had happened.

When its head hit the ground, I saw what had killed it. In the left side of its head was an arrow. Looking up from where the arrow had been buried, I saw Unni putting his bow away.

I was sure glad to see him. "Thanks for the help!" I told him as I got up.

Unni just nodded his head in acknowledgement as he checked the monster's corpse. "This-ah creature is-ah called an edepitenc," he stated grimly. "The venomous-ah bite of an edepitenc-ah this big is deadly ta any man."

We headed back to the campsite together silently. Unni was probably upset that I had so recklessly abandoned my watch post to fight a dangerous monster alone in the forest. I could have been killed. I felt embarrassed by my actions and tried to apologize to Unni, but he told me to forget about it.

Daylight was beginning to peek over the horizon. My watch was over. We saw Okin coming out of his tent, dressed and armed. He was starting to pack up.

When we reached the site, Okin asked us, "What-ah happened?"

Unni shrugged. "Just collectin' Lorenz, here."

Unni was being vague and covering for me. I decided to tell Okin like it was. "There was a creature in the woods hanging around the camp. I went out there to see what it was, but it was too much for me. Your brother had to come to the rescue. It was a big edepitenc."

Okin's eyes widened and he looked at his brother Unni, who nodded. "I see," replied Okin.

We quickly put out the fire, broke down the camp and got back on the main road going south. We figured we should quickly get back on the trail before something else came out of the woods towards us. In a few more minutes, we had reached the road and were traveling.

As usual, Okin led the way, followed by Unni and myself. I immediately took out my map, asking the dwarves to stop for a second to check out our location. We looked at the map. The "X" showed we were about a mile north from the bwasan leaves. We headed for my destination, but we hadn't even been walking for five minutes before Okin stated pointedly, "I'm-ah hungry!"

"What if we ate when we get to the forest? Can you wait that long?" I asked him. A mile wasn't that long to wait.

"I suppose-ah so." He sounded a little disappointed.

The early morning was damp and brisk. Droplets of dew hanging on tree leaves and blades of grass caught the sunlight and sparkled. Birds chirped and sang their morning songs. This world was very beautiful when there weren't giant things trying to kill me.

Soon, we had reached the path where we were supposed to turn off into the forest. It was clear that we needed to go up the path up ahead to reach the meadow where the bwasan leaves were found. On each side of the path, the trees seemed to be getting shorter. They were of varying colors, but they didn't match what Thiek and the book had described the bwasan leaves to look like. The leaves were supposed to be squared-shaped red leaves with bluish veins. Most of the leaves here were rounded and light green.

We continued up the path, checking out the trees along the way. As Unni and Okin were busy scrutinizing the leaves of some of the plants, I saw up ahead a patch of a different color.

"You guys go ahead and eat. I'll be back."

"A'right!" Okin shouted and pulled out some wrapped morsels from his pockets to much on.

"Where are-ah you going?" asked Unni.

"I think I see something." I told him and headed further south towards the area where I saw the bright colors.

I looked around to make sure no one was watching me. I didn't even want Unni and Okin to see what I was doing. I felt a little bad for sneaking around like this, but I figured Thiek's quest didn't really have anything to do with them. I quickly entered between the trees, brushed aside the branches and reached the colorful patch.

I had found the red and blue bwasan leaves. I was amazed at how different they were compared to all of the other leaves and colors around them. I quickly picked a handful bwasan leaves from a few of the more vibrant branches and put them safely away in my bag. When I'd finished, I headed back to where the brothers were resting.

I didn't realize how long I'd been. They had already finished eating and were brushing the crumbs from their clothes when we saw me coming. Okin asked me, "Where are-ah we goin' now?"

"I need to see a friend of mine now that I'm done here." I said to Okin.

"Where is-ah this-ah friend?" asked Unni.

"He lives on the way into town. You guys want to come?"

The two of them thought about and said something to each other in their language. Finally, Okin replied, "No, we need-ah to go into town-ah for-ah some-ah supplies."

"Okay," I said to him. "Why don't we meet tomorrow morning? That way we can meet up and work out what to do next."

We had started walking back towards the main road while having this discussion.

"That-ah soun's like a plan," said Unni, agreeing happily.

"We'll-ah be betta prepared-ah this way, afta gettin' what-ah we need," said Okin approvingly.

When we reached the main road, we headed back north. We talked about many stories of adventures that they had been on. They spoke with great enthusiasm about the many incredible things they had faced and how they'd almost kicked the bucket a few times in some of their tougher journeys. They exclaimed about the exotic places their travels had taken them and the great food they'd eaten.

Unni was really excited as he shared his stories. He was so excited in fact, that a couple of times he almost tripped over his feet as he gestured animatedly. As I listened to them, it made me excited about journeying, fighting, exploring, and making money too.

Thinking about what we might face made me a bit nervous, but seeing how much we had successfully gone through the last few battles reassured me a little.

"Why don't we go into town and look for adventures together?" I suggested to them.

"Yeah, let's-ah do that-ah! We'll-ah go into town-ah to fin' people looking-ah for-ah travelers!" agreed Okin.

By this time, I was at the path that led back to Thiek's house.

"What a house!" the two brothers exclaimed at once, admiring the size and architecture.

"Yeah, my teacher lives here. So, I'll see you guys tomorrow morning. Where should we meet?"

"How about-ah tha local tavern?" asked Okin.

"That sounds good!"

So the three of us said our temporary goodbyes, shook hands, and went our own ways.

I walked up the path towards my teacher's house. My instincts told me that Thiek was waiting for me at home. The sun was shining bright, high in the sky for noon. When I was halfway up the path, Thiek opened the front door to welcome me, as if he knew exactly when I was returning. He had a smile on his face.

As I got closer, I bowed my head respectfully. He gave a nod back. While I climbed the front steps, he suggested to me, "Tell me about your journey over some hot tea?"

"Yes, of course. Thank you," I replied.

I followed him into the large room. Everything looked the same. As I entered the kitchen, I took off my backpack, pulled out a chair and sat down, stretching out my tired legs.

Thiek went to the stove and grabbed a teapot which was sitting on the burner, already steaming. He brought it to the table where there were already two wooden teacups set up. He poured the hot golden tea into each cup, one for each of us.

"I'm glad to see you back safe," he said as he set the pot back down on the stove. "I suggest that when we finish our tea, you get some rest, then study and prepare your spell if you haven't already. So, tell me about your journey."

I grabbed the cup set aside for me and blew on the hot drink to cool it down. I started with telling him about how I had walked down the path and saw the two dwarves engage in battle with a creature I'd never seen before.

As I went through each part of the journey, Thiek listened intently and asked questions whenever he wanted more details. He was particularly curious about the monsters and the mysterious old house. Before I knew it, the sun was beginning to set, as we had talked the whole afternoon away. Thiek had by now prepared dinner, we were eating and I had said everything I could about the journey.

"Well, that was quite a tale. But for now, you should go and prepare your spell!" he said.

So I gathered my things, thanked him for dinner and headed towards my room. When I left, he was occupied with cleaning up the kitchen after making dinner and didn't pay too much attention to me.

I felt a little disappointed by our talk. He asked a lot of questions, but he didn't react in the excited way that I thought he would have. Maybe I said something or did something wrong? I didn't let it bother me too much. I had to focus on working on my spell. As I thought about this, my pace quickened and before I knew it, I was at the soul room.

Now learning cigam and many other new skills, Lorenz is well prepared to accept his next challenge.

However, one trial he may not be ready for is the meeting with his fated nemesis. Let's hope Lorenz will be able to handle him when the time comes.

The wicked Davian, now more powerful than most others in the land, is still unaware of this new potential threat to his reign.

His only focus remains finding what will make him ultimately the most powerful cigamian alive.

What flames will rise when the two finally meet?

fstpulp.com

draegongrey@wordpress.com

@draegongrey(twitter)

Draegongrey@yahoo.com

Facebook

Linkedin